THE COLD TRAIL

THE COLD TRAIL

PAUL EVAN LEHMAN

CUTTING EDGE

ISBN-13: 978-1-954840-09-6

Published by
Cutting Edge Books
PO Box 8212
Calabasas, CA 91372
www.cuttingedgebooks.com

CHAPTER ONE

JIM RANDALL was being followed. Although he rarely caught sight of the horseman behind him, Jim knew that the fellow had been camping on his trail ever since he had passed through the Cherokee Strip. Up to that point he could not be certain, for the news which had brought him from Montana so disturbed him that he had little thought for anything else.

He had come swiftly and steadily, taxing to the utmost the endurance of his horse. This morning he had crossed the Colorado and another two days' ride should see him in Briscoe, where a talk with Lewis Dunham should resolve the questions which had tortured him ever since the receipt of Dunham's terse note. Jim could remember that letter almost word for word.

> *Dear Jim,*
>
> *After quite a search of your father's effects I finally found your address. Sorry I could not notify you sooner, although in any case you could not have arrived here in time.*
>
> *Your father died suddenly two months ago as the result of a bullet wound, and I suggest that you come to Briscoe as soon as you can.*
>
> > *Very truly yours,*
> > *Lewis J. Dunham.*

Died suddenly as the result of a bullet wound! His father, so far as Jim knew, had not an enemy in the world, yet he had been

1

shot. By whom? And why? These were two questions to which he must have answers.

His weary horse stumbled, lunged in an effort to recover, and went down. Jim kicked free of the stirrups in time to avoid a fall and helped the animal to its feet only to find that it had pulled a tendon. Fortunately the town of Juniper was less than a mile ahead, and Jim walked the rest of the distance, leading the horse. The rider behind him drew closer, then passed at a sharp lope without even making an inquiry. He was a short, swarthy man and a stranger to Jim.

Randall led the horse to the livery corral in Juniper, took off the gear and rubbed him down thoroughly, afterwards placing him in the care of the hostler for feeding and rest. Briefly he debated buying another mount, finally deciding to take the stage which was due to arrive within the hour and which, after laying over for the night, would depart early in the morning for Cottonwood Junction, where it made connections with a branch line to Briscoe.

Dusk was falling when he left the corral and went to the hotel. Securing a room, he washed up, learned that supper would be served as soon as the stage arrived, and went outside. He looked carefully about but the short, swarthy man who had followed him was not to be seen. He was wandering aimlessly along the street when the stage rumbled into town and drew up at the station a short distance away.

Jim strolled to where it stood, arriving just as two passengers alighted. Easterners, he judged them. The man was middle-aged, of average build and appearance, and Jim gave him but one glance. The girl was different.

It wasn't altogether that she was extraordinarily pretty; it was rather her bright, eager expression which attracted him, the grace of her movements, the light which shone in her eyes, the complete wholesomeness of her. Although she had evidently travelled far she appeared fresh and expectant as one on the threshold of adventure and intrigue and mystery; and as she stepped to the ground her glance fell on Randall and he unconsciously returned her smile. Instantly her attention went elsewhere and he knew that to her he was but part of the scenery, a detail in the vast panorama of the West which she had come to view.

The man, who appeared to be her father, spoke briefly with the agent then picked up two valises and started along the street, the girl at his side. Jim saw them enter the hotel.

He had finished his supper and was leaving the dining room when they entered, and once more her glance found him, lingered momentarily, then moved on past him. Although he could not know it she was saying to herself, *This is a cowboy. How tall he is! And how well he wears his colorful clothes and that big gun at his side!*

Not once since he entered Juniper had he seen the short, swarthy man.

He went into the lobby and sat there for an hour, asking in his mind the questions he must ask Lewis Dunham, wondering about the big ranch his father had owned and which Jim, as his father's heir, would now inherit, regretting that he could not have been there when they laid John Randall to rest. Save for a few scattered cousins with whom they had long since lost contact, Jim and his father had been alone, Jim's mother and sister having passed on some years before.

That night he went to bed late and, much later, still thinking about the sudden death of his father, the man who had followed him—and the girl who had got off the stage—he finally fell asleep.

Early the next morning he paid for passage to Cottonwood Junction, went to the livery corral and arranged for the care of his horse, then stuffed his gear in a gunny sack and tossed it atop the coach. He ate breakfast with the girl and her father, listening in silence to their inconsequential talk, finding a strange pleasure in the girl's soft voice. Afterwards, when the two had entered the stagecoach, he climbed to the seat beside the driver. For the first few miles of the trip he kept glancing behind him, but caught no sight of a following horseman and concluded that the short, swarthy man was unaware that he had taken the stage.

They had their noontime meal at a station half way to Cottonwood Junction, which place they were scheduled to reach that evening. A night there and Jim would take the branch line to Briscoe while the girl and her father, he assumed, would continue south and east to San Antonio. Briscoe was a small town and held no attraction for tourists.

They arrived at the Junction at dusk and Jim carried his gear to the hotel, registered and went to supper. He noticed the notation on the register above his own—Alonzo Lane and daughter, Linda. Linda Lane; it held the note of a soft-toned bell. He repeated the name to himself. Linda Lane.

He met them again as he was leaving the dining room and this time he knew the girl's smile was for him. It was a frank, friendly smile and for a moment he felt regret that this was probably the last time they would meet.

He killed time as best he could, postponing retiring as long as possible. His restlessness had increased as the distance to Briscoe had diminished, and he knew he would not sleep well. He had been a month on the trail. Dunham's letter had probably taken as long to reach him, and it had been written two months after his father's death. A lot can happen in four months. If his father had been murdered, as he suspected, the trail of the killer would be stone cold.

It was nearly midnight when he finally sought his room. He removed his coat and boots and gunbelt, opened the window and stretched out on the bed in the darkness. He lay there for a long time, thinking, wondering. The sounds of the town's night life died, a great silence descended, the air came through the. window cool and soft. He dozed.

He awoke suddenly but without movement, his breath coming as evenly as when he had slept. The transition from sleep to wakefulness was instant and complete and every sense was alert. The moon had risen and even within the room objects were faintly discernible. The mirror above the dresser shone palely and he could see the white pitcher on the washstand. Without moving his head he slanted a glance towards the window. Black against the moonlight were the head and shoulders of a man. He was leaning with his left elbow on the sill; the right arm was extended and Jim could see the blue steel of the Colt which was coming down to a level.

Jim rolled quickly, making a complete revolution and striking the floor just as the gun roared. His own weapon was on the chair and he sent a probing hand towards it as another shot thundered. The bullet tore through the bedding and mattress and struck him in the side. Failing to find the gun, Jim seized the chair and pulled it over; his fingers found leather and he drew the colt, rolling instantly to another position.

He fired upward through the bed, estimating the location of the window, and heard the crash of glass as his lead found the pane; then a third shot sounded and he knew the would-be assassin was still there and unhurt.

To remain on the floor would mean death. Once more he rolled, to bring up against the door. Springing to his feet, he tore it open. It shuddered to the impact of another slug and splinters stabbed him in the face. He squeezed through and leaped to one side of the doorway. The panel splintered under another slug and he heard the lead thud into the opposite wall.

His intention was to descend the stairs, rush outside and catch the man as he descended the ladder; but even as he turned towards the stairway he saw by the light of the hall lamp another dark figure peering at him over the top step. The light glinted on the barrel of a Colt and he sprang sideways as the flame of the discharge stabbed at him.

His leap was an instant too late; he felt a blow on the side of his head as though he had crashed into a brick wall and the whole world seemed to explode. Instinctively he fought unconscious-ness—knew vaguely that he was firing his gun as rapidly as he could thumb the hammer, although no sound reached him above the roaring in his head. He saw a door open on his left and saw the girl, Linda Lane, standing in the entrance.

She had thrown a dressing gown about her and clutched it with tense, white fingers, holding it closed at the throat. Her eyes were wide with horror and fright, her lips were parted in an exclamation that he had not heard, her face was plaster-pale. Just for an instant he saw this, then her arm was extended towards him and blackness engulfed him as he stumbled towards her.

He awoke to find himself on a bed. There were several people in the room and one of them was cutting away his shirt. Standing beside him and holding a basin of water was Linda Lane. He heard her say in a low, tense voice, "He's awake, Doctor."

A voice said, "That's too bad. I've got to fish for that bullet."

"Linda, you'd better leave the room," came another voice which Jim judged belonged to her father. "This is going to be too much for you."

She shook her head, her gaze still on Randall. "No; the doctor needs me."

"Better hang on to something, son," advised the doctor. "This is going to hurt a bit."

The girl put the basin on the floor and, kneeling, took one of his hands between her own as though to force some of her own youthful strength into his lax muscles. The brown eyes were filled with pain and pity. Jim felt the stab of the probe. Moisture gathered on his forehead but he kept his gaze on Linda Lane and the smile remained on his lips. He saw her quiver and felt the nervous pressure of her hands. When he finally fainted he was still smiling.

When it was over and Linda and the doctor were alone with the unconscious patient she spoke anxiously. "Do—do you think he'll get well?"

"Get well? Him? Miss, he's built like the rock of Gibraltar. Of course he'll get well. He'll wake up in the morning yelling for steak and hashed brown potatoes."

"Why did that man try to shoot him?"

The doctor shrugged. "Out here somebody's always trying to shoot somebody else. They generally succeed. You see, we haven't reached the point yet where there's a policeman on every corner and a law banning the carrying of lethal weapons."

"The—the man outside?"

"As dead as Julius Caesar. Good riddance, if I'm any judge of appearances. There was another on a ladder outside the boy's window. Took a shot at him while he was in bed, I suppose. Got away clean. Well, I'll drop around in the morning and see how he is."

"Shall I stay with him?"

The doctor smiled. "If you want to. He probably won't wake up for some time, though. After what you've been through I'd suggest that you let me give you a sedative and then go to bed."

"I'll go," she said reluctantly, "if you're sure he won't need me. But no sedative, please. We leave early in the morning."

The doctor left and Linda gathered her luggage together and carried it to the room her father had engaged for her. The next morning on her way downstairs she looked through the open doorway at him. He was sleeping deeply, quietly. Linda tiptoed to the side of the bed. She saw that in repose his face was strong and handsome, the hair above the bandage touseled and curly. She rested her hand lightly on the dark curls in a gesture of farewell. In another hour she would be on the stage bound for Briscoe; he, she assumed, would continue on the main line to San Antonio. Their paths had crossed momentarily only to part again. She realized suddenly that she was sorry.

Randall did not awake crying for steak and hashed brown potatoes; to the contrary, he found sitting up in bed a painful operation and when he finally got to his feet he was momentarily overcome with a wave of weakness. He set about dressing and was in the midst of that chore when the doctor entered the room.

From the man of medicine Jim learned that the slash in his scalp had required six stitches to close and that the wound in his side, while of the flesh variety, was serious enough to cause trouble unless properly cared for. Despite this, Jim flatly refused to return to bed.

"If I do, I'll be here for two weeks. I'll stiffen up like an old cow and get so weak I won't be able to stand. No, Doc, I'm getting up. Help me with this shirt; I got to catch the stage for Briscoe."

"You'll have to run pretty fast," said the doctor shortly. "It left an hour ago. Better take my advice and get back in bed. Confound it! I don't see how you stubborn fellows keep alive."

"Probably because we're too stubborn to die. That fellow who was at the head of the stairs—did he keep alive?"

"Not with three slugs in his chest."

"Three! I don't even remember firing them. Who was he?"

"Nobody seems to know. He's down at the undertaker's if you want to take a look at him."

Jim paid him for his services and when he had gone crossed the hall to the room he had originally occupied. His possessions were intact, which fact confirmed his belief that robbery was not the motive for the attack. It was his life they wanted, nothing less; but why?

Walking stiffly and painfully, he went downstairs, got some breakfast and immediately felt better. The town marshal came in while he was eating and asked some questions. Jim told of the short, swarthy man who had followed him and learned that the fellow had entered the Junction in advance of the stage. The marshal did not know him and he had not been seen since the attack.

Jim spent the day alternately prowling about the town and resting. He viewed the remains at the undertaker's and was sure he had never seen the man before. He was also short and swarthy and somewhat like the other in appearance, but Jim knew that he was not the one who had followed him. A brother, perhaps.

That evening he had the dressings on his wounds changed and persuaded the doctor to replace the bandage about his head with a small pad held in place by adhesive. He slept soundly through the night and awoke refreshed and stronger, and when the stage left for Briscoe he was on it.

Noon found him at his destination. Removing his gear from the top of the coach, he carried it into the stage station and dropped it into a corner.

"Howdy, George," he greated the agent "Mind if I leave my stuff here for an hour or so?"

The agent looked at him coldly. "Help yourself," he said, and went outside. Jim stared after him in wonder. He had known George Finch ever since he was a boy, yet the man had treated him like a stranger.

His wonder grew as he walked along the street towards the bank his father had founded. Men whom he had called friends in the past nodded curtly or changed their courses to avoid him. Tightlipped, Jim strode up the steps of the squat brick building and halted abruptly at the door. On it was a sign which read CLOSED.

He turned slowly and looked about him. What had happened here in Briscoe since his departure a year before? Apparently the town was unchanged; there was the same dusty street with its uneven plank sidewalks and hitching posts and tie rails, the same drab buildings, the same people. But there had been a change, certain if subtle. This was his father's town; John Randall had founded it and nourished it and had taken a huge pride in it. A year before men would have stopped Jim to shake his hand and exchange news and banter with him; now they avoided him as though he were a leper.

A sign on a modest building across the street caught his eye. It read JASON RUDD, Real Estate. Jason Rudd had been the bank's bookkeeper. Jim squared his shoulders and crossed to the office, assured that from Rudd he would at least learn the reason for the bank's closing.

Rudd was a little man of middle age with thick-lensed glasses and thinning hair. He was seated at a high bookkeeping desk and favored Jim with a slight nod. Jim put an elbow on the desk and spoke shortly. "What's wrong with the bank, Jason?"

Rudd inspected the point of his pen, tried it on his thumb nail. He answered slowly, choosing his words. "After your father's death it was thought best to close it."

"My father was killed, wasn't he? Who did it?"

Rudd looked at him for a moment, his face blank. "I think you'd better talk to Mr. Dunham about it. He's expecting you."

"Where can I find him?"

"On the Box D. He stays there most of the time, now that the bank's closed."

Jim said bluntly, "You don't seem in a mood for answering questions today, but tell me this: What have I done to make you and the rest of the town treat me like a strange dog?"

Rudd made a quick gesture of denial. "That isn't so! You haven't done a thing, Jim. It's just that—well, you'd better talk to Mr. Dunham; he'll explain everything."

There was nothing to be learned here. Jim turned abruptly and walked out. He got his gear from the stage station and went down to the livery corral. He knew the liveryman too, but the fellow had no greeting for him save a cool nod. Jim didn't even try to be pleasant; crisply he bargained for a horse and paid for the animal in cash. The liveryman was shamefaced and embarrassed. John Randall, Jim remembered, had set him up in business.

Jim saddled up and rode away. Out in the broad valley the air was crisp and clear and he felt a slight rise in spirit. Diagonally to his left, miles away, were the buildings of his father's Star ranch; those of Dunham's Box D were located diagonally to his right and were about the same distance from him. Tucked in a pocket of the hills directly ahead was the quarter-section his father had deeded to him on his twenty-first birthday, just before his departure for Montana to hunt wild horses. It was a pretty place, well located and with good water, and one day Jim would have stocked it and built up a herd of cattle; now, however, the Star would be his and he would have his father's cattle.

He rode slowly, favoring his weak side and the sore head which was prone to throb under too much jolting, and it was after three when he drew rein outside the Box D ranch house. As he swung to the ground, Lewis Dunham came to the door and spoke coolly. "Hello, Jim. You made good time; I didn't expect you for another week. Come in."

Jim followed him into the big living room and took the chair indicated by Dunham. Here too the greeting lacked warmth, and Dunham had been one of his father's best friends. Jim came to the point at once. "You know what I'm here for, Lew. Tell me about it."

"It isn't easy," said Dunham slowly. "Not even after four months. But it's got to be done and I suppose I'm the one to do it. Jim, the truth of it is that your father put all of us in an awful mess."

Jim's face hardened. "I'm listening."

"Well, you know your father. In many respects he was a fine man, genial, openhanded, everybody's friend. He founded the bank and we made him president. It turned out to be a mistake. He would grant loans to anybody who handed him a hard luck story. If he took a note, he'd mislay or destroy it. If we protested, he'd say that he knew the man and that his word was good enough. When Jason Rudd protested that he couldn't keep his books straight, John told him to charge any apparent shortage to his personal account.

"I knew in a general way what was going on but I didn't go to the bank any more than was absolutely necessary and had no idea of what was to come. Rudd finally called the matter to my attention and I had a talk with John about his looseness. I told him we'd have to have something to show for all the money he'd lent, and he offered to give us his note, secured by a mortgage on the Star, for any discrepancy.

"That was fine; we could put the books in order and know where we stood. I told Rudd to make a careful audit and draw up the note and mortgage for John's signature. This he did. It took him a week. He drew up the note and the mortgage and John signed it. Brent Wood witnessed his signature. It was after banking hours and they left him alone in his office. He seemed in good spirits, confident that the men he had trusted would make good. It was the last time anyone saw him alive. Brent found him the next morning. He was sprawled across his desk with a bullet hole in his head."

"Murdered!" said Jim tightly.

Dunham shook his head. "I'm afraid not. Beside him on the desk was the revolver he kept in a desk drawer. It had been fired once."

Jim came to his feet. "You're trying to tell me—!"

"Yes. I couldn't believe it at first. He had never seemed to me to be the kind of man who'd take that way out. Then Rudd showed me the note he had signed and I could understand. Jim, the amount was *fifty thousand dollars.*"

Jim stared at him for a moment. "That's a lot of money, but the mortgage would have covered it."

"Just about. Unfortunately, that wasn't all. The Sheriff's Office took charge. We went through John's papers and the few records he kept. He had destroyed most of his correspondence apparently, for we couldn't even find your address. But we did find a letter he'd overlooked. It was from a Chicago stock broker. We contacted him and found that John had made some unfortunate investments. Not large ones, but undoubtedly there were other transactions with other firms. There must have been to account for such a huge amount. We carried quite a bit of cash in the vault at all times because of gold purchases, and Rudd had struck his balance as of the first day of the audit. After your father's death a new audit was ordered. A week had passed, but in that time an additional shortage of some twenty thousand dollars had accrued. The conclusion was obvious."

"Are you accusing my father of stealing?" cried Jim hotly.

"I'm making no accusations at all, Jim; I'm merely stating facts. And those facts are from the Sheriff's Office and can be verified. Seventy thousand dollars of the bank's money was gone; your father was found to have been speculating; then he committed suicide. There was only one conclusion to draw. Maybe that's brutal, but you're his son and entitled to know the facts. I believe you're man enough to face them. We closed the bank to prevent a run, foreclosed on the mortgage and sold the Star to the Acme Cattle Company, and thus realized fifty thousand dollars. We divided it up among our depositors and called it a day."

Jim slowly sank back into his chair. He was sick at heart and felt as though the weight of the building rested upon him. "That's why they won't speak to me," he said dully. "That's why they avoid me." He shook his head as though to clear it. "I don't believe it. I can't. Dad was a fighter; he wouldn't quit."

"I believe that he shot himself on the spur of the moment," said Dunham. "I imagine that when he saw that note before him and knew that there was another twenty thousand not represented in it, he realized for the first time how deeply he had involved himself and how impossible it would be to redeem himself. He burned his correspondence in the office fireplace and finished it. The letters from you and the broker I found jammed behind a desk drawer where he evidently overlooked them. Two months had passed since his death, but I wrote you at once."

Jim got up. "As it stands, I owe the bank twenty thousand dollars."

"That's wiped out. You can forget it."

"No I can't. I have the place Dad deeded to me; I'll stock it as best I can and turn the profits over to you until the whole sum's paid."

Dunham eyed him thoughtfully. "I was hoping you'd want to sell that place, Jim. I was ready to make you an offer."

"It's not for sale, Lew."

"Think it over. Frankly, you can't make a go of it here at Briscoe. Folks will hold your father's actions against you and make it as difficult for you as they can. That's only human nature. If you sell out to me you could make a start elsewhere."

"I'm staying, Lew. My father's life was his own and what he did with it is between him and God; but I'll not have him remembered as a thief. Thanks for your frankness and goodby." He turned and walked from the house.

Wearily he swung into the saddle and started for Briscoe. Bitterness welled up within him. He had come to Briscoe shocked by the death of his father but determined to avenge his murder, and he had found—this!

The sun was low when he rode into the town, tired and weak and, at last, hungry. And as he walked his horse along the street he saw a rider dismount before a store and go inside. Buried in his thoughts, the man had vanished before the realization reached Jim that this man was short and swarthy and very like the man who had followed him south.

The realization galvanized him. He reined to the hitching rail before the store, dropped from the saddle and ran swiftly up the steps, hoping to come upon the fellow suddenly and surprise him into some betraying word or act. He bolted through the doorway, then checked himself abruptly to avoid colliding with a customer who was coming out. Instinctively his arms went about the other to preserve their balance, and in the same instant he knew that the body he clutched belonged to a woman. At first he could see only the top of a new cream-colored Stetson, then her head was tilted upward and he found himself looking into a pair of startled eyes.

"You!" cried the girl.

"You!" exclaimed Jim.

"I thought you—" They said it in unison, then stopped abruptly. Jim withdrew his arms, his cheeks reddening, and Linda Lane, amusement replacing surprise, laughed.

"Shall I finish it? I thought you'd gone to San Antonio."

Jim glanced over her shoulder. The short, swarthy man had disappeared but at Linda's elbow stood a slim, handsome man in his early thirties who wore the garb of cowman with considerable aplomb. The eyes which observed Jim were narrowed slightly and there was an almost imperceptible curl to the lips beneath the neatly trimmed moustache.

Linda turned. "Mr. Randall, this is our foreman, Mr. Dirk."

The man nodded. "Howdy," said Randall. He noticed that she had called him by name and concluded that he wasn't the only one who had peeped at the hotel register.

Linda said, "Do you live in Briscoe, Mr. Randall?"

"I was born and raised here."

"Then we'll probably be seeing you quite often. But your wounds! The doctor said you'd awaken calling for steak and potatoes, but I thought—"

"I'm lots better, thanks."

Jim heard a flurry of hoofs in the street behind him and knew that the short, swarthy man had slipped out the rear door, circled the store and was now hotfooting it out of town. Stepping to one side, he waited until Linda and Dirk had mounted their horses and ridden away, then re-entered the store and went about ordering tools and supplies.

The storekeeper was cool and polite, and Jim confined himself strictly to business. This man also had benefited by his father's generosity, but like the rest of the townsfolk preferred to forget past favors in the light of recent events.

Jim left his purchases at the store and rode to the livery corral, where he bargained for and bought a used wagon and a set of harness. Stripping the saddle from his horse, he hitched the animal to the vehicle, drove to the store and loaded his supplies.

Dusk was gathering when he headed out across the range for the homestead at the base of the hills.

CHAPTER TWO

RANDALL DROVE slowly to avoid jolting as much as possible, his mind busy with the appalling story related to him by Lew Dunham. It was impossible for him to reason coherently; his brain was numb from the shock of the thing and within him a voice was shouting that what had happened was utterly impossible. Yet the evidence was damning, the facts apparently conclusive. He would, of course, check Dunham's story from every angle, but in his heart he knew that he must be prepared to accept it. Dunham would not make such statements on hearsay or guess.

The sun had disappeared and purple dusk was gathering when he crossed the ridge which marked the boundary of his homestead. The scene before him was beautiful even in its desolation, with the log cabin and corrals outlined against a background of liveoak and pine, the little stream bubbling joyously from the spring, the grass, tall and lush, where cattle could browse the whole year round, the range being protected from wintry blasts by the barrier of the hills.

As he approached the place he saw with a feeling of satisfaction that everything was in good repair. The roof of the cabin had been freshly sodded, there was glass in all the windows, the corral had been strengthened. When he entered the house it was to find the stove still warm, but his momentary surprise was dispelled when he remembered that the homestead had been used by the Star as a line camp. He went about preparing a meal, for he had not eaten since morning.

Refreshed and relaxed and at last able to think coherently, he rolled a smoke and settled down to another review of the disclosures which Dunham had made. Questions which had formed in his subconscious mind presented themselves for answer. Why had his father, who had courageously fought man and beast and the very elements without faltering, chosen to take the easy way out? How had he happened to overlook that one damning letter telling of his unfortunate investments? Why had he elected to keep his defalcations secret instead of frankly presenting them as the reason for his suicide? Why had he left no word of explanation or justification for the son he loved?

And, on top of these, *why had the short, swarthy man attempted to murder that son?*

He had found no answer to any of the questions when he finally turned in, but something kept telling him that there was a logical solution to the whole thing and he was resolved to find it.

Morning found him astir early, and after breakfast he went about some necessary tasks. He cleaned the cabin thoroughly, cut fresh boughs for the bunk, spent several hours getting in a supply of firewood. Now that the Star had passed into the possession of the Acme Cattle Company, he would have to build fence for the cattle he intended to buy. These, he determined, must be the very best he could procure.

He was cutting fence posts when he saw a bunch of riders top the ridge and come sweeping down the grade towards the homestead. Two men and a girl rode in front, and he recognized Linda Lane and the man she had introduced to him as Jeff Dirk. Then he recognized a third and instinctively his hand fell to the butt of his Colt. He was the short, swarthy man who had tried to kill him!

Dirk raised his hand and they pulled down to a walk, and now Jim saw that the man on the other side of Linda was Briscoe's marshal, Jeb Mosley. Behind them, in addition to the would-be killer, were three hard-looking characters. The whole bunch halted a dozen feet from Jim and he raised his hat to Linda and said, "Good morning, Miss Lane."

She answered him gravely, a troubled look on her face. Jeff Dirk said, "You figure on settling here, Randall?"

"Yes."

"Didn't bother to get the Acme's permission, did you?"

"No."

"Then you'd better be moving on."

There was a provoking sneer on Dirk's lips and his eyes glinted. Sure of his ground, he had brought Linda along so that she could witness Randall's discomfiture. Jim guessed his object at once and glanced at the girl. There was a little frown of anxiety on her forehead.

"I like it here, Dirk. Reckon I'll stay."

"You got another think coming. This is Marshal Mosley of Briscoe. Tell it to him, Jeb."

The marshal spoke shortly. "Dirk's foreman of the Acme. You heard him order you off the place. Better go peaceable, Randall."

"Suppose I don't, Jeb?"

"Well, I'm the law around here. I'd have to put you off. Reckon there are enough of us to see that you go."

"Jeb, you're only a town marshal; your authority doesn't extend to the range. But even if it did I'd still refuse to go. You see, I happen to own this quarter-section."

"Own it!" scoffed Dirk. "You own it about as much as I own Patagonia. This land belongs to the Star; always did. The Star was bought by the Acme."

"If you'll take the trouble to look up the records at Hartsville," Jim told him coldly, "you'll find that this quarter-section is part of a grant by the State of Texas to my father and was deeded by him to me on my twenty-first birthday. Right at the moment it's you who are trespassing, not me."

The change in Dirk's expression was a bit comical. Gloating triumph was transformed suddenly into consternation and doubt. "Is that right, Jeb?" he asked the marshal.

Mosley scratched his head. "Danged if I know. Might be, at that."

"It is," confirmed Jim. "All you got to do is look up the records. I'll remind you again that you're trespassing. If you've finished your business, you can get off my land."

Dirk's rage and humiliation was reflected in his flushed face. Behind him his four followers watched for a sign that would send them into action, but with the marshal and Linda present there was nothing left for Dirk to do but withdraw as gracefully as he could.

"I'll give you the benefit of the doubt until I know for sure," he said tightly, and swung his horse about. "If you're lying, we'll be back."

Linda turned her mount to follow Dirk, but before she did so she found Jim's gaze upon her and smiled at him. Later, when the marshal left them and headed for Briscoe, she said, "Do you think it'll be necessary to look up that deed, Jeff?"

He had recovered his poise but not his good humor. "It'll be necessary to check up on everything that bird says. He's probably just as bad as his father was."

"His father?"

"You wouldn't know, of course. He was one of those big shots. Owned the Star and was president of the bank. He made off with seventy thousand dollars and when he saw they were going to check up on him he shot himself."

"Oh!" exclaimed Linda faintly, and suddenly found the morning not so bright as she had thought it.

Back at the homestead, Jim worked steadily at his job of post cutting, stopping only long enough to eat. All that day and all the next he worked, cutting trees, trimming them, snaking the logs to the cabin for sawing into the proper lengths. Then came the job of post-hole digging, then the firm setting of the posts. On the fifth day he drove to Briscoe for wire, and by the end of a week the fence was completed.

Jim did not know where he was going to get the cattle he wanted. The Star and the Box D were the nearest ranches and both had some good stock. Jeff Dirk was foreman of the former outfit and Jim was reluctant to have any dealings whatever with the man. Also, Dirk might queer any deal he tried to put through with the Acme. Jim decided to see Dunham and rode over when the fence was up. Lew met him on the ranch house gallery and Randall stated the reason for his visit. "I want to buy some purebreds; eighteen or twenty young cows and a couple bulls. Have you anything in that line you'd sell me, Lew?"

Dunham regarded him thoughtfully. "So you're determined to go on with cattle raising, are you? I'm afraid, Jim, that you'll never make a go of it."

"Whether I make a go of it or not, Lew, should make no difference to you. I want some brood stock and I'm willing to pay you cash. How about it?"

"I'm afraid I have nothing for sale, Jim. I'm expanding myself, which is why I'd like to have your place. I need every head of stock I have, especially brood stuff."

Jim turned abruptly and started for his horse. No use to waste time here. When he mounted, Dunham called and came down from the gallery. "If you're really bent on staying, Jim, there's a rancher named Turner a few miles this side of Hartsville who has some good young stock. You might make some sort of deal with him."

Jim thanked him and rode away. At the moment he had no inclination to take Dunham's tip. Lew easily could have supplied him with what he wanted, but the man did not want him to succeed and made little attempt to hide his animosity. Jim rode into Briscoe and ate dinner at the hotel. As on the former occasion, people avoided him or, when forced to recognize him, spoke coldly. Their conduct hurt and served at the same time to strengthen Jim's determination to pay his father's debt. He inquired of several merchants where he could purchase some stock, and one of them suggested Amos Turner of Hartsville. Dunham's suggestion had evidently been given in good faith.

Since it was a full half-day's ride to the county seat, Jim set out at once. As he was about to swing into the saddle he paused to stare at a passing horseman. Low in spirit as he was, the sight brought a smile.

Even in this land of horses it was quite evident that Jason Rudd was no equestrian. He sat his saddle stiffly and awkwardly and his attire was little suited to the occasion. He wore a rusty black suit and string tie, his long coat tails draped over the cantle and the legs of his trousers rubbed above his skinny calves by the stirrup straps. On his head was a derby hat with a rolled brim, and thick-lensed glasses were perched on his thin, hooked nose. Jim watched until he saw Rudd leave Briscoe and head out into the valley, then stepped into the saddle and set out for Hartsville.

It was dusk when he dismounted before Amos Turner's ranch house. Turner was a lank man with a persimmon face who listened to Randall's wants and then surprised him by stating that he had just what Jim needed. Delighted, Randall rode out on the range with him to examine some of the stuff and found the animals entirely satisfactory. They were Herefords, young and sturdy, and the price Turner named was a fair one considering their high quality. The deal was soon closed and Turner persuaded Jim to remain at the ranch over night, promising to furnish enough men to drive the stock back to Briscoe. Jim turned in that night with the satisfying knowledge that he had made a bargain ....

It took Jason Rudd almost as long to reach the Star ranch house as it had taken Jim to travel the thirty-odd miles to that of Amos Turner, for he walked his horse the entire distance and dismounted frequently to rest his lame muscles and rearrange his clothing. In due time he tied to the hitching post before the house, dusted himself off and, mounting the gallery, rapped on the door. It was opened by Linda.

Jason removed the derby. "Ah, good evening, Miss Lane. It is Miss Lane, isn't it? I'm very glad to know you. I'm Jason C. Rudd, until recently bookkeeper at the Miners and Merchants Bank at Briscoe. I would like to see your father if he's at home."

"Do come in, Mr. Jason," said Linda. "Father's in the living room."

Jason entered the big room and she took his hat. Alonzo Lane was seated in the late John Randall's favorite easy chair carefully perusing a stock journal in an effort to acquire some knowledge of the animals entrusted to his care by the Acme Cattle Company. He got to his feet, was introduced by Linda, and waved Rudd into a chair. Linda went out into the kitchen, leaving them alone.

They chatted of inconsequential things for a while, then Rudd cleared his skinny throat and said, "As I told your daughter, Mr. Lane, I have been until recently the bookkeeper of our local bank. When it was closed after the death of our president I opened a real estate office. The venture has not proved very lucrative and in any event is one which does not appeal to me. My heart, Mr. Lane, is in accounting work and it is because of that that I called on you today."

Lane was interested. "Yes?"

"Yes. Mr. Lane, you are a man of managerial ability, otherwise the Acme Cattle Company would not have engaged you as their manager. Now the community needs the services of a bank and the organizers of such an institution will most certainly profit under good management. The building can be bought or leased at a very nominal figure. Mr. Lane, I am anxious to see you reopen the Miners and Merchants Bank of Briscoe."

"Really?" Alonzo Lane was genuinely surprised. "That's very nice of you, Mr. Rudd, and I am flattered. But such an undertaking would involve the investment of a considerable sum of money, and I assure you that I am not by any means a rich man. I merely manage the Star; I don't own it."

"But you are in touch with the owners; in very close touch, I should think. In all likelihood the company relies greatly on your judgment. I am quite sure that if they could be induced to finance the project they would find their investment a profitable one indeed. As bookkeeper I am in possession of figures showing the profit to be realized, and the bank would be of real service to them I'm sure. You would be our president and I would take care of the accounting end. I believe Mr. Lewis Dunham, our former vice-president, could be induced to assist you in the direction of the affairs of the institution, and you would continue here as manager of the Star."

"It's an interesting idea," said Alonzo Lane. "Very interesting, indeed. I have had some banking experience, having held a position with a trust company in Philadelphia before coming out here. But you speak of profits; I was under the impression that the Briscoe bank had failed."

"Merely because of our unfortunate choice of a president. He was very lax. When his defalcation was discovered he—ah—took his life. I am quite sure that with you in office we need anticipate no such unhappy ending."

"I think I can guarantee that, Mr. Rudd. You say you have some figures showing the earnings of the bank?"

"I have," said Jason Rudd, and proceeded to produce certain documents showing the amount of gold taken from adjacent mines and handled by the bank and disclosing the profits on certain transactions involving its purchase and shipment. The accounts of merchants were summarized and the amounts of payrolls stated.

They conferred for an hour or more, Lane making copious notes to be incorporated in the letter he promised to write the company's lawyer in Philadelphia; and at the end of that time the little bookkeeper was persuaded to remain for supper and Lane left him smoking a cigar while he went to the kitchen to inform Linda that they were to have a guest.

"Be nice to Mr. Rudd," he advised her. "He has offered me an excellent opportunity and I want to make him feel at home."

So Linda went out of her way to be pleasant to the man with the thick-lensed glasses, and Jason Rudd was humbly grateful and declared that never before had he enjoyed such delicious cooking. Lane promptly invited him to remain overnight in order that they might go into the figures more carefully, and Jason, after a bit of polite hesitancy, accepted.

After supper the three of them went out on the gallery and sat in the gathering dusk, and presently Lane left to write the promised letter. The little bookkeeper, tactfully aided by a dutiful Linda, lost some of his shyness. Darkness fell and the stars came out in all their blazing glory and Jeff Dirk, watching glumly from the bench in front of the bunkhouse, cursed under his breath and wondered just what this insignificant little man had that he hadn't.

Jim spent most of the next day selecting the stock he wanted, helping to cut out and corral the animals; then, not wishing to start the drive in the evening, he spent another night at the Turner ranch.

They started the next morning, Turner aiding Jim and the two borrowed hands until the main trail was reached. Here the sourfaced rancher wished Randall good luck and turned back and Jim pointed the little herd towards Briscoe. One of the cowboys, known as Kansas, was stationed on the right flank well up near the head of the bunch; the other, named Carp, took a similar position on the left flank. Jim rode drag. One of the bulls showed an inclination to stick to the trail and was used to point the herd.

They moved off at a smart walk and after the first few miles experienced no difficulty in keeping the animals to the trail. Jim followed in their dust, free from the cloud of worry which had hung over him for the first time since his arrival in Briscoe. In the broad backs and shaggy hides before him he saw the nucleus of the herd which was to restore the good name of his father and serve as the beginning of a prosperous career. They nooned at a stream previously selected by Randall, and at the end of the day made their camp on the range where the grass was good and the water sweet.

Although the animals had been hazed along at a brisk clip they were not overly tired, and Jim and Kansas found it necessary to ride herd on them while Carp prepared supper. They took turns watching through the night, and at five in the morning their breakfast was over and they were on their way again.

The sun of the second day was low when they entered Briscoe and moved slowly along the street towards the valley range. The animals had begun to tire now, and it required the efforts of all three drivers to keep them moving. The closeness of the buildings on both sides of them, the pedestrians on the sidewalks, the shying of horses at hitching rails all seemed to disturb the Herefords; they were restless and excited and showed an inclination to bolt into passageways or vacant lots.

People on the street stopped to watch, and those in the stores came to the doorways. To Jim their faces were cold and unfriendly. They considered him the son of a thief and a suicide and they did not want him here. Jim recognized many of them as he passed: Jason Rudd, peering through his thick glasses from the door of his real estate office; Lem Fisher, the owner of the hotel; Lew Dunham, standing beside Lem, his features as stolid and unreadable as those of a wooden Indian.

The shouts of Kansas and Carp and a sudden commotion at the head of the column drew Jim's attention. He peered through the dust and saw at once the cause of the disturbance. Into the far end of the street had turned four horsemen; they were riding abreast at a full gallop, their hands rising and falling as they quirted their horses to greater efforts. Randall's first thought was that they were cowboys racing for one of the saloons, then he recognized them as the four who had been with Jeff Dirk the day Jim ordered him off his land and he knew their action was not the result of chance.

He spurred along the flank of the restless Herefords calling, "Hold 'em, boys!" and headed at a gallop for the approaching riders, jerking the rifle from beneath his knee as he rode. Fifty yards in advance of the cattle he pulled to a halt and swung the weapon to his shoulder. He did not fire for fear of further alarming the Herefords, but his action was significant enough and the dust churned as the four sat back on their reins and came to a plunging stop. Directly in front of Randall was the short, swarthy man, and it was he whom the rifle covered. This man, Jim was sure, was the one who had tried to murder him while he slept, but he had no proof that this was so.

The man said angrily, "What's the idea, Randall? You figure you own the town, too?"

Jim lowered the rifle, holding it so that he could bring it to bear the instant one of them went for his gun. He said, "You're not blind; you saw these cattle."

"Supposin' I did? Cattle belong on the range; not in a town."

"I'm getting them there as fast as I can. Pull off to one side and let them by." The man glared at him defiantly, and Jim made a threatening motion with the rifle.

Jeb Mosley came out into the street, his hard gaze on Randall. "What's goin' on here? Randall, put up that rifle."

Jim didn't obey. "Cattle have the right of way when they're on a drive, and it's your job, Mosley, to clear the street for them."

"I don't need you or nobody else to tell me my business. Seems to me you're a mite too quick on the draw. Get back to your cows and get them under control before they do some damage. Panhandle, you and your men pull over and keep your horses quiet."

So the short, swarthy man was known as Panhandle, thought Jim as he backed away. He kept his gaze on the fellow and his rifle was still ready. Panhandle growled an oath, but the marshal made an imperative gesture and he reined to the right and led the way to the side of the street. He called to Jim, "You're mighty brash when you got a gun on a feller."

Jim didn't answer him. Carp and Kansas had their hands full and needed his help. The restless animals had spread all over the street, and Carp had been forced to take Jim's place in the drag to prevent the animals turning and stampeding. Jim edged up to the lead bull and got him straightened out, talking softly and taking care to make no sudden move. Riding close to the animal, he started him along the street; the second bull fell in behind, then a couple of the cows. Kansas joined Carp in the drag and began hazing the Herefords forward. At last the whole bunch was in motion once more, and Jim turned and rode back along the flank. He shoved the Winchester back into its boot.

The drag was passing when he reached the group of four who sat their saddles at the edge of the street, and he was about to order Carp and Kansas back into their positions when his horse gave a startled leap that nearly unseated him. For a few moments there was confusion as he fought to regain control of the animal, and Carp and Kansas were hard put to keep the cattle moving. When he had quieted his mount he wheeled to see the man Panhandle coiling his quirt.

Hot anger boiled up in Jim and spilled over. He leaped his horse straight at the fellow and Panhandle, suddenly realizing that Jim's fist was balled and ready to fly, dropped the quirt and snatched out his gun. Jim left the saddle in a dive and his extended hands caught the fellow by the wrist and his momentum dragged the other from his saddle. The two of them landed in the street and before Panhandle could recover Jim twisted his arm savagely and he dropped his gun with a howl of pain.

Jim came to his feet dragging the other after him. He said through his teeth, "See what you can do when I don't hold a gun on you!"

The fellow leaped forward and swung, but Jim ducked beneath the flying fist and planted a solid right into the man's stomach. He grunted and his guard came down. It was too good a chance to miss. Jim stepped in and landed a left cross, then followed with a straight right to the mouth. The man staggered back a few feet and sat down in the dust.

Beyond Panhandle, Jim could see the three other men still sitting their saddles, watching. The sudden ending to the fight had paralyzed them momentarily, and his own gun was out before they could make a move. He said, "I'll take you on one at a time, with fists or guns; but not the three of you at once."

Jeb Mosley came striding across the street, his hand raised. "No shootin'!" he shouted. "Jim, put up that gun. You other fellers stay froze."

Jim watched them for a moment, then pushed his Colt back into the holster and walked a few feet up the street, where a man was holding his horse. He took the rein, thanked the man shortly, mounted and rode after his cattle. By humiliating Panhandle before his companions and the whole town of Briscoe he had made a mortal enemy, but he was not dismayed. These people, he determined, were not going to kick him around like a stray dog, and if anybody wanted a fight he could have it for the asking.

Night was near at hand when they halted the cattle near a water hole five miles beyond Briscoe and prepared to camp for the night. The worst of the drive was over; they had pushed the animals hard and had covered four-fifths of the distance to the homestead. Before noon of the next day the little herd would be under fence. It was a heartening thought and Jim was almost lighthearted as he rode in for supper.

The weary cattle finally bedded down and watches were set. There was a strong possibility that Panhandle and his friends might make trouble and Jim was determined not to be caught napping. Carp was to watch from eight to eleven, Jim from eleven to two, and Kansas from two to five. Under this arrangement Carp and Kansas would each have six hours' unbroken sleep. Jim would have two periods of three hours each.

When Carp awakened him the night was silent and cool. "Them cows is sure enough spooky," said the cowboy. "You'd think that after bein' drove the way they was the danged critters would be willin' to rest. They ain't."

"They haven't got over Briscoe yet." Jim told him. "Also they're on good range and smell others of their kind. They're young and restless and want to be on the move. No matter how good pasture is, a cow seems to think there's better somewhere else."

"Ain't much difference between them and humans after all, is there?" grinned Carp, and sought his blankets.

Jim saddled up and rode out on the range. Some of the Herefords were lying down, but most of them were moving about and he had to watch them constantly to see that they didn't stray. He walked his horse, singing softly, counting their dark shapes to make sure they were all here. The minutes dragged into an hour, two hours. The campfire had died to a bed of embers and both Carp and Kansas were sleeping soundly. Then, from some point to the west of Jim, came a sudden burst of gunfire.

Jim jerked his pony to a halt, senses alert. There were no houses in that direction, just open range. What did the shots mean? They couldn't have been more than a mile away. He sensed movement about him and saw that all the cattle were on their feet. One of them bawled and immediately others joined in the chorus. Several of them started at a shambling trot away from the bunch, and Jim was forced to spur hard to head them.

"Carp! Kansas!" he shouted.

For several minutes he was busy holding the herd intact, then the two cowboys came riding up. "What's wrong with the danged brutes?" asked Kansas petulantly as they rode circle on the herd.

Jim explained about the shots. "I don't know what they meant. If they had been closer I would have thought Panhandle and his bunch were trying to stampede the herd."

"Listen!" said Kansas suddenly, and pulled his horse to a halt. Jim also drew rein. From the west came a low, insistent rumble. "What's that?"

"Sounds to me like a stampede," answered Jim. "And headed right for us. We better get these cows away from here. Hey, Carp!"

Carp had also heard, and he answered at once.

"Point 'em up! Find that lead bull and head him north. Kansas, give me a hand."

"Jim, we'll never hold 'em. Look at the danged critters!"

"We got to get them out of the way of that stampede. Get busy, I tell you!"

They set about a task which was hopeless from the start. The stampeding animals were but a short distance away and the earth trembled under their pounding hoofs. The Herefords refused to remain bunched and Jim finally called both men back to help him drive them. The three riders spread out in the rear of the frightened animals and lashed them forward at a right angle to the course of the stampede, hoping to clear the rushing juggernaut that was bearing down on them. Both Herefords and horses were pounding on at a full gallop, but despite all efforts to hold the cows on their course Jim saw one animal after another bear away to the east, terrified by the rumbling threat on their left.

And then in the starlight they saw the first ranks of stampeding cattle. Like a swift black flood they rushed towards Jim and his Herefords; the air was filled with the clash of horns and the pound of hoofs. They would never make it. Jim saw the last of his animals bolt off at a tangent and with despair in his voice ordered his two men to cut for it.

Half an hour later their horses pawed desperately up the steep sides of a ridge and they halted on its top to watch the black flood roll past. Starlight shone on dark heaving backs and tossing heads, and when at last they had passed the thick dust rose to obscure the sky. For a long while Jim and his men sat their saddles in silence. When the sounds of the frantic flight had died in the distance and the dust had settled somewhat, Carp spoke.

"Cow critters shore are ornery. Here we are on a calm night with not a sign of storm or thunder or lightnin' and nothin' in God's world to stir 'em up, and all at once two, three thousand of 'em go plain loco and come bustin' straight for our camp. Wonder what started 'em?"

Jim told him. "That big herd was started by gunfire. I heard it off to the west. I figure it was Panhandle and his pals. They knew we'd be on guard against them, so they did their stampeding from a distance."

"Shucks, he ain't had time enough since your run-in with him at Briscoe," said Kansas. "Them cattle were gathered before they were stampeded."

"It was no secret that I was looking for cattle; I told several people about it before I was sent to Turner. Panhandle and his bunch heard of it and set the thing up while I was gone."

"That jigger sure must have it in for you, Jim."

"It won't do him any good. The cattle are scattered, but they all wear Turner's brand and can easily be identified. It will mean work, but we'll get them back."

They had supplies on their saddles. They built a fire, had a smoke and turned in for the rest of the night. Before dawn they had their breakfast, and when they had finished eating Jim said,

"You boys have kept your part of the bargain; you might as well get started for Hartsville."

"We'll scout around with you until noon," said Kansas. "Ought to be able to pick up some of them for you."

They started as soon as it was light, following a course taken by the stampeded cattle, and were on Lew Dunham's range before they sighted any of their cattle. They cut them out and drove them as they crossed the range and by noon had recovered both bulls and two-thirds of the cows.

Jim, greatly encouraged by their success, thanked Turner's men, paid them generously and watched them ride back towards Briscoe. The animals were quite docile now and he had no difficulty driving them without help. He headed them for his pasture at a plodding walk, planning to get these animals behind fence and then to ride in search of the others. His enemies had succeeded only in hampering him.

He wondered as he rode whether this was the work of one man who was determined to ruin him, or, as Dunham had suggested, a concerted effort on the parts of a number who were taking their resentment against his father out on him. The stampede had been started by Panhandle and his pals, he felt sure; but he had a hunch that somebody bigger than any of these was behind the thing. Dunham? He just didn't know.

It was dusk when the cattle toiled up the rise which marked his boundary. They passed over the crest and moved down the far side. Jim followed them and saw the cabin and corral ahead of him. He stared across the backs of the cattle, looking for the fence in the growing darkness. Then he reined in with an exclamation of dismay. Along the line where the fence had been were regularly spaced piles of smouldering ashes and twisted, tangled, fire-blackened wire. He spurred around the cattle, bitterness welling up within him.

He knew what he would find even before he reached the line. He knew now that the stampede of the night before had been staged to gain time—time to drag the posts from the ground and cut the wire and set the fires that would nullify days of labor.

And that wasn't the worst of it. He had paid three times the price of ordinary stock in order to get purebreds, and now he had no means of keeping them segregated from the range stock of the Acme and Lew Dunham.

CHAPTER THREE

H<small>E DROVE</small> the Herefords down the slope to the spring. There was nothing he could do but hope that the good range and water would hold them close to the homestead until his fence was rebuilt. The corral was too small to use for them, and if they were penned in it he would have to feed them and water them by hand.

In any event he would have to rebuild the fence. If he wanted to raise purebred stock these good bulls and cows must be kept off the range where they would surely crossbreed with poorer strains. The building of a new fence would mean another week of back-breaking work, but this he did not mind. It was the cost of wire and staples which hurt, for he had spent every cent he felt he could afford to buy the cattle. He must have some reserve to fall back on, to keep him in food and clothing and tools until his herd began to produce.

It was too late to start cutting fence posts; the best thing to do would be to eat a good supper, turn in early and be up at dawn. He started for the house and as he rounded the front corner he saw a man riding towards the cabin. He waited and presently recognized Lew Dunham. Lew pulled up before him and said, "I see you got your cattle; but what happened to your fence?"

Jim told him briefly, watching the man carefully to observe his reaction. Lew listened quietly, then nodded. "I told you folks would resent your staying here. The Acme wants your place for a line camp and I want it for the spring and for winter grazing. I'll pay you a fair price for the cattle and fifteen hundred for the quarter-section."

Jim shook his head. "There's only one price you could name that would tempt me. That's twenty thousand, four hundred dollars."

"Twenty thousand! Jim, you're crazy."

"No. I aim to get out of this homestead the amount my father was short plus interest from the date of his death. If the place is worth that much to me, it's got to be worth that much to anybody else that wants it."

Dunham made an impatient gesture. "I told you to forget that twenty thousand. Except for the sale of the building itself, the affairs of the bank have been wound up."

"I'm not interested in the affairs of the bank, Lew. Regardless of what the law says, my father died owing twenty thousand dollars and I'm going to pay it. My father was a good man, Lew; he treated people square and nearly everybody in Briscoe owed him at one time or another. When this thing came up, they forgot all about that. I aim to pay them off and then tell them all where they can go."

Dunham stared down at him, and now there was a flicker of admiration in the cold eyes. "Damned if I don't believe you mean it! You'll be butting your head against a stone wall, but I wish you luck. You'll sure need it. And if you find the going too tough, don't forget to give me first chance to buy you out."

He wheeled his horse and rode away and Jim went into the cabin to prepare supper. The mystery of his father's defalcation and death had risen anew to plague him; imperative as it was that the fence be rebuilt, it was even more imperative that he check the story Dunham had told him. In any event the cattle must be permitted to shift for themselves; the matter of an extra week or so would make little difference.

Early the following morning he saddled up and rode through Briscoe and to the county seat at Hartsville, arriving there in the evening. He immediately sought out the county attorney at his home and had a long talk with him. The attorney's story was identical with that of Dunham except that it was more detailed. In his mind there was no doubt of John Randall's guilt, no extenuating circumstances whatever. He took Jim to his office and gave him the cancelled note and mortgage. Jim scanned the signatures on both instruments carefully and was forced to admit that the writing was that of his father. But then the question of the authenticity of the documents was not in question; it was the elder Randall's suicide which caused the doubt and perplexity. Jim just couldn't believe that.

"There were some personal possessions I'd like to have," he said. "Letters and little gifts from my mother that he treasured, her picture, his watch and a few other things."

"The sheriff has the watch and all other personal belongings we found, Mr. Randall, I know of no letters or pictures; he must have destroyed them with the other correspondence."

"How about the furniture in the house? Was it covered by the mortgage?"

"No. It belongs to you. There was no chattel mortgage."

"Under the circumstances, getting it might be quite a job. Still it's mine. How about a court order turning it over to me?"

"A good idea. We'll run over to Judge Morgan's house."

The order was duly secured, after which Jim thanked the attorney and went in search of the sheriff. The lawman readily delivered the few personal effects he had in his possession, but knew nothing of any letter or picture.

"Only letters I know anything about were the two Lewis Dunham found. One was from you, the other was from that stock broker."

Dunham again. Funny that just those two key letters had been found. Greatly perplexed, Jim went to the hotel for the night and started for Briscoe early the next morning. He rode directly to the homestead, hitched up the wagon and drove over to the Star. It was an all day ride, and when he arrived the crew had just finished supper and were lounging about the bunkhouse. Seeing

Panhandle and his pals among them, Jim kept his hand close to his gun; but they chose to ignore him, so he dismounted, tied at the hitching post and knocked at the door.

Linda opened it and looked up at him gravely, and although there was no welcoming smile neither was there hostility in her gaze.

"Is your father in, Miss Lane?" he inquired.

She nodded and stepped to one side and Jim stepped into the livingroom. Alonzo Lane was seated in his father's favorite chair and a short distance from him Jeff Dirk sprawled on the sofa. Both men were evidently awaiting supper.

"What is it, Randall?" asked Lane coolly.

"I drove around to get a few of my belongings," answered Jim, and handed him the court order. Lane read it quickly, his face reddening.

"Why, you can't take the furniture!" he cried. "We need it here. It was purchased along with the ranch."

"The mortgage covered only the stock and buildings and equipment; there was no chattel mortgage on the furniture."

"But I tell you we need it! It—it's preposterous! We can't eat and sleep on the floor!"

"That's a court order, Mr. Lane. If you refuse to obey it, I can call in the sheriff."

Dirk got up and came over to him, his attitude belligerent. "Look here, Randall, you can't take this stuff without due notice. Mr. Lane must have time to replace it."

"I don't like that word 'can't', Dirk. It's mine and I can take it or break it up for firewood or do anything I want with it. In any case it's no business of yours. Better keep out of it."

Dirk was a proud, arrogant man, and with Linda looking on could not tolerate domination by a man whom he had belittled to her. "I'm foreman of the Star and I'm making it my business!" he snapped. "I'll not be dictated to by the son of a common crook."

Jim's fist hit him with the sound of an ax on a sodden log. Red rage multiplied his strength and the blow would have dropped an ox. Dirk was hurled backwards a full six feet, striking the floor with a thump which jarred the building and sliding his length after he hit.

Alonzo Lane cried out harshly and Jim heard a little suppressed scream from Linda as he strode forward, fists clenched, to stand over the stricken man with the hope that Dirk would find strength to get up so that he could hit him again. But Dirk lay where he had fallen, and after a moment the mist before Jim's eyes dissolved, the ringing in his ears ceased, his taut muscles relaxed.

He turned quickly to Linda, who stood with her hands at her throat in much the same attitude she had assumed that night when he had been shot before her eyes. "I'm sorry," he said quietly. "Not sorry that I hit him, but sorry that I had to do it here. My father was not a common crook and nobody's going to say he was in my presence. I'll take what I want and get out. I want the chair my father liked and a few other things. The rest you can use as long as you need them."

She didn't answer, but went quickly to where Dirk lay and knelt beside him. After a moment she got up and went into the kitchen, to return with a basin of water and a towel. Alonzo Lane had retreated into a corner from where he glared at Jim with all the ferocity he could muster.

Randall picked up the heavy chair and went out with it, placing it in the wagon. The men were still in front of the bunkhouse, but made no move to stop him, evidently relying on Dirk to summon them if they were needed. Jim went inside again and, ignoring Lane and his glare, took a few other articles his father had treasured and put them into the wagon. Keeping an eye cocked towards the crew, he drove out of the yard and back to his cabin.

The next morning he drove to Briscoe to buy the wire he needed for his fence. All but a few of his Herefords had strayed from the quarter-section, but there was nothing he could do about it at the time. The people of Briscoe still spoke to him coolly or not at all, and he treated them in like fashion.

To this atmosphere of cold animosity Jim found one exception. Brent Wood, the young man his father had placed in the bank, had secured a position as clerk in one of the stores and was waiting on Jason Rudd when Jim entered. At sight of him, Brent came around the counter and shook his hand with every evidence of sincere liking. His action touched Jim so profoundly that for a moment he could not speak.

"Brent, you're the very person I wanted to see," he said at last. "This thing about Dad—I just can't believe it. What can you tell me?"

Brent sobered. "It hit me awfully hard, Jim. He was just like a father to me. I don't know what to think of it; my heart says one thing and my head another. Jason, here, asked me to witness John's signature on a note and a mortgage, and we went into the office. He wasn't smiling; he was as sober as a judge. Later I thought that maybe he was hurt because the thing was considered necessary. You know, when a man puts his name to a mortgage on everything he has in the world it—it sort of hurts. Anyhow, he signed both mortgage and note, and I witnessed his signature. We didn't hang around; I signed and Jason gathered up the papers and said something about it being a mere formality, and we left him sitting there. The next morning—well, I guess you've heard the rest."

"And you think he shot himself, Brent?"

"That's where my heart said no and my head said yes. It wasn't like John Randall to run away from responsibility; but the wound was in the right temple and there were powder burns, and it was his own gun. I know that. And when it came out that the note was for fifty thousand dollars—well, I just had to believe that he'd committed suicide. But I told them then and I'm saying it again that John was the victim of some clever broker who robbed him blind; and I swear I don't believe he realized he was in as deep as he was until that note was handed to him for his signature. The only way I can figure it is that in his remorse he just took out the gun and finished it."

"That the way you think, Rudd?"

Jason turned a pair of mournful eyes on him. "It was a very sad affair, Mr. Randall; very sad indeed. John was an excellent man; they don't make them any better. None of us dreamed— even I didn't know just where we stood until I finished the audit, so confused were things. In a way I blame myself for the tragedy. If I had insisted upon an accounting earlier the whole unfortunate affair might have been avoided."

"There are some things of his missing: a picture of my mother and some letters from her that he had kept. Do either of you know what became of them?"

They shook their heads. "The sheriff took charge of the search," said Brent. "You'll have to see him. Jim, what are you going to do?"

Some people came into the store and Jim saw Brent and Rudd nod to them, but he did not turn. He said, "I aim to stay right here until I've paid back the twenty thousand he still owes. I can't believe he deliberately stole it, but I'll pay it back just the same, with interest. And while I'm about it, I'm going to dig into the thing until I'm satisfied that the story I've been told is the true one."

"Good for you!" approved Brent. "And if I can help, you'll call on me, won't you, Jim?"

Jim said he certainly would and turned away, and now he saw that it was Linda Lane and Jeff Dirk who had entered the store. They must have heard his last statement, for they were both looking at him. The twist to Dirk's lips was more pronounced than usual, and his dark eyes glinted maliciously; the girl's expression was unfathomable. Jim touched his hat brim and started past them, but Dirk stepped forward and halted him with a curt gesture.

He said in a low voice, "I guess you know that I'll pay you back for that sock in the mouth," he said.

"You're welcome to try it any time you feel lucky, Dirk."

"Just wanted you to know that I'm not overlooking it. I don't jump a man when he's off guard and I never brawl in the presence of a lady." He said this loud enough for Linda to hear and Jim flushed.

He turned his back before Randall could find an answer, and Jim went out of the store inwardly fuming. Dirk had taken the opportunity to show him up before Linda and for some reason not yet clear to him he resented it. Always, it seemed, he must appear before her in an unfavorable light. First in a gunfight, then as an arrogant land owner who had ordered her off his property, and finally in a brawl in her own home. Now Dirk had rubbed it in for her benefit. He told himself fiercely that what she thought, what anybody thought, didn't matter a tinker's damn, and knew immediately that in her case it did matter.

He ate dinner at the hotel, returned to the store to buy the wire and started back to the homestead. On the way out of town he saw Dirk in close conversation with Lew Dunham. In his present mood he was ready to suspect anything and anybody. Dunham wanted his homestead and he had quarrelled with Dirk; were the two joining forces against him?

He arrived at the homestead late in the afternoon, unhitched and corraled his horse and stored the reels of wire in the shed. As he was about to enter the cabin he stopped. On the door was tacked a sheet of paper with printing on it. He read the note once and swore.

THIEVES AND THE SONS OF THIEVES ARE
NOT WANTED IN BRISCOE. GET
OUT IN 24 HOURS OR TAKE THE
CONSEQUENCES.

Randall tore the paper from the door, strode angrily into the cabin and lighted the lamp. Then he sat down at the table and, spreading the sheet out before him, studied it. So they were determined to get rid of him. Who? Dirk and his four hoodlums suggested themselves at once. The printing could have been done by Dirk, for the words were correctly spelled and the letters properly formed and spaced. But if this order to leave were connected with the attempt on his life, Dirk was out, for he had not even known of Jim's existence at that time.

Who then? Dunham? He was an educated man and could have printed such a sign. This could be just another attempt to get rid of him so that Dunham could use his quarter-section. The objection to this was that Dunham surely knew by this time that Jim would not be scared away.

He pushed the paper aside with an exclamation of disgust. If they thought that he would pay any attention to this notice they were very mistaken. He'd stay and face those threatened consequences.

The vigilance he had partly relaxed was now renewed; he saw to it that the cabin was sound against assault and that his weapons were ready at hand. Instead of sleeping in his bunk he spread his blankets behind the stove; then, putting out the light, he slipped out into the darkness and led his horse into the leanto behind the cabin.

For a long time he lay pondering the problem. His danger had started with Panhandle who had followed him south; but certainly the plan to kill him while he slept had not originated with Panhandle. The man was a typical rough, strong of body but not overly intelligent, and Jim had never before seen him. Somebody must have hired him to murder Jim. But why?

The more he thought it over the more convinced he became that possession of his homestead was not the motive for his removal. It just wasn't worth the price. The one who did the hiring would be as guilty as the actual killer and would lay himself open to blackmail by that person. A thousand-dollar homestead wasn't worth that. Yet what other reason could any one have to desire his death?

That reason reached him at last, and it came with such astounding force that it raised him up in his blankets. Perhaps his presence in Briscoe was feared! Perhaps his unknown antagonist was apprehensive that he might not accept the story of his father's suicide as readily as had the law accepted it! Perhaps it was feared that the son might dig deeper than had the sheriff and might uncover something that smelled to high heaven!

Jim sat there on his blankets, his eyes wide. That was it! By the eternal, that was it! Somebody had laid a very clever plot which included the disgrace and death of John Randall, and now that somebody was afraid that the son would not accept surface facts and must be removed before he was able to discover just what had happened.

Small but significant details began to forge to the front of Jim's brain. There was his father's failure to leave some word of explanation; the burning of the correspondence, even to the letters from his wife; above all, the destruction of her picture, if it had been destroyed. John Randall would have died with that clasped to his heart. The conviction which Jim Randall had held all the while asserted itself with a strength that would not be denied. John Randall had not committed suicide; he had been murdered.

Jim got up and paced the floor. Why had his father been murdered? To cover up the theft of another? The mortgage and note denied that; both had been signed by his father as an acknowledgment that fifty thousand was the amount of the shortage.

He puzzled over the matter, eager, as alert as a hound on a fresh trail, convinced that at last he was getting close to the truth. Dunham had been vice-president of the bank; Dunham knew of his father's laxity in money matters, his careless loans, his contempt for written records. If Dunham could have convinced his father that the money he himself had appropriated had been tossed away in loans by Randall! But fifty thousand dollars! Even without records John Randall would have known the amount to be out of all proportion to what he had lent.

Jim didn't sleep; dawn found him still trying to fit the pieces of the puzzle. He washed in cold water, fed his horse, then prepared and ate some breakfast. Mind more composed, he sat down to review facts and theories from the beginning. When he had done so he came to the conclusion that there must be no guesswork. If he were to save the good name of his father and pin his murder on the right one, he must have a firm foundation on which to build.

He saddled up and rode to town, pushing his horse, and arrived there at ten o'clock. Dismounting before the hotel, he went inside and asked a cold-faced clerk for Lem Fisher, the proprietor. Lem came out and at sight of his visitor his face lost its professional smile.

"Good morning," he said without enthusiasm. "What can I do for you?"

Randall wasted no words. "Before my father's death I suppose he spent some nights in town, didn't he?"

"Why, yes; he did for a fact, Jim."

"Ate his meals and slept at your hotel?"

"Yes. Towards the end he spent most every night here."

"Probably used the same room regularly?"

"That's right. The best in the house; number one, in the front."

"Lem, I'm looking for some letters and a picture of my mother he had. Did he leave them in his room?"

Fisher's stare was blank. "No, he didn't. Fact is I never seen anything but his clothes and a newspaper or two."

"Mind if I look the room over?"

"Not at all. But the sheriff went through everything and you're just wasting your time." Fisher got the key and they went upstairs together. The room was just like any other hotel room, with the customary bed, dresser, washstand and chair and a closet in which to hang garments. Jim looked through all the drawers and into the closet and found them empty.

He thanked Fisher and left the hotel. He crossed the street and entered Jason Rudd's real estate office. Jason, perched on his high stool before his bookkeeping desk, gave him a nod and an owlish stare.

"Jason," said Jim, "do you have the keys to the bank?"

"Yes, I have." He smiled faintly. "Thinking of leasing it?"

"I'd like to look around inside. Those letters and the picture have got me guessing. There's just a chance that they've been overlooked."

"I can assure you that they haven't, but you're welcome to look." Rudd slid to the floor and took a key from the desk drawer and his derby from a nail on the wall. "Come along," he said.

The interior of the bank building was cold and musty and cobwebby, and its dank air settled over Jim like a pall. He stood for a moment looking about him at the dusty partition with the grilled windows and the huge vault behind it, at the desk where Jason Rudd had officiated, at the two doors lettered respectively PRESIDENT and VICE-PRESIDENT.

"This way," said Rudd, and stepped towards the former.

He opened the door and they went in. There was a desk and a swivel chair, another chair with a straight back, a hat-rack and umbrella stand, and a filing cabinet with the drawers pulled out. Jim went to the cabinet and examined it carefully; then he moved it to one side so as to look behind and beneath it. He found nothing and went over to the desk. One by one he removed the drawers and peered into the openings they left. He found nothing.

He crossed to the fireplace. There were ashes in it, the ashes of paper, crumbled by poking and stirring. Jim squatted on his heels and moved the pile to one side, then started sifting the ashes through his fingers. He stopped to examine a small corner of dark cardboard, then rose slowly to his feet with the fragment in his hand.

"What is it?" asked Jason curiously.

Jim showed him the bit of cardboard. His eyes were narrowed and his breath came quickly. "A bit of my mother's picture," he said.

"I see. So he did burn it with the rest of his papers."

Jim did not answer, but he knew that the picture had not been burned by John Randall. To have burned her picture would have seemed like sacrilege to him. Somebody else had burned it, and the knowledge that this was so confirmed the belief that he had held from the beginning. He said shortly, "My father didn't commit suicide; he was murdered."

Rudd blinked his surprize. "Murdered? Impossible. Why, I saw him! The pistol was right beside his hand and there were powder burns on his face."

"Jason, that doesn't mean a thing. The killer could have held the gun close to his head when he fired, and he could have put the gun on the desk by my father's hand. In fact, that's just what he would have done if he had wanted it to look like suicide." He whipped out his Colt. "You saw where the gun was lying. I want you to take the position my father was in when he was found, and I want you to put the gun in the position it occupied."

Jason took the gun, holding it gingerly, looked carefully at the top of the desk, then deliberately laid the Colt on its surface. He sat down in the swivel chair, moved it slightly, then leaned forward until his head and part of his chest rested on the desk. His right hand rested between the gun and his head, and his left arm dangled.

Jim examined his position relative to the gun carefully, then asked, "You're sure this is exactly the position?"

Rudd blinked up at him. "I'm positive. There isn't much doubt is there?"

"Yes," said Jim tightly, "there is. Father's hand rested between the gun and his head. That's all right. But the butt of the gun is pointed away from him, towards the edge of the desk. I should think that with a bullet through the brain both hand and gun would drop together; but if he let go the gun first, it would have fallen between his head and his hand. He'd almost have to *throw* the gun to have it land where it did."

Rudd sat up, allowing his right hand to remain on the desk. "I see what you mean, but it's dreadfully far-fetched, Randall. He might have thrown the gun; reflex action, you know. Why, he could have even dropped it and have it land where it did."

"You're right. But remember the butt is pointing away from him." He picked up the gun and pointed it at his own temple. "Dad's hand was lying palm upward; if I drop the gun and let my hand fall in the same way the butt would point inward."

Rudd shook his head. "I still say it's far-fetched. Too much so to base a theory of murder on."

"It's good enough for me," Randall told him shortly.

"Well," said Rudd doubtfully, "you might tell the sheriff about it and see what he thinks."

"I don't think I will. In his mind the case is settled; it'll take more than this to persuade him to reopen it. No, I'm not going to notify him. And I'd like you to keep my theory to yourself; don't give a hint of it to anybody."

"Of course not. I still think you're being swayed by sentiment. I never dreamed—"

"That it could be murder? I have. In fact, that's all I have dreamed about. Well, let's get out of here."

They went out of the building, Jason locked the door and Jim gazed after him as he crossed the street to his office. Randall wasn't sure of his next move, but one thing was certain: he must dig into the past, trace Lew Dunham's movements on the evening and night his father was shot. Five months ago. The coldest kind of trail.

He went to the hotel for dinner, pondering the matter while he ate. When he had finished he sought out Brent Wood and questioned him. It had to be done carefully so that Brent would not suspect. Brent knew nothing about Dunham's movements on the night in question, but he did remember that Lew had not been in the bank that day.

Jim made a circuit of the town, forcing himself to be civil with men whom he knew looked at him with scorn and for whom he felt a deep contempt. He made his inquiries casually, but could find nobody who remembered seeing Dunham that afternoon or night.

The better part of the evening was consumed in this manner, and it was after sundown when he started for the homestead. He rode now with his chin in the air. His father was not guilty; he was no thief, no suicide. The burning of his mother's picture, the position of the gun were both feeble clues but to Jim convincing ones.

Remembering the warning which had been tacked to his cabin door, Jim approached the place warily, leading his horse and circling the house before entering. It was dark and empty and he lighted the lamp before taking the horse into the leanto. He off-saddled and went to the shed for a forkful of hay and a measure of grain. He put the grain in a box where the horse could reach it, tossed the hay into a corner, then returned to the shed with the empty measure and the pitchfork.

They hit him as he entered the dark shed; how many of them he could not tell. The fork was snatched from his hands and they fell on him in a body and in silence, clinging to his arms, his legs, about his waist, climbing upon his back. Blows rained on him from every direction as he struggled furiously to shake them off.

He struck out savagely and felt his fist thud home; he lashed out with his feet and felt the shock of his boot striking at every kick; he bent and heaved and twisted, but they clung to him like leeches and their blows fell on his head, his face, his shoulders and stomach.

His gun was jerked from its holster and tossed aside, and by sheer weight of numbers they dragged him to the ground and smothered him beneath them. Not once had he heard a voice; nothing but the hard, labored breathing of men working furiously at a difficult task. Then his foot found the pit of a stomach and a grunt of agony was forced from the man as he was hurled backward.

There was a crushing blow on Jim's head and he went limp.

He recovered consciousness slowly, painfully, the blood throbbing in his head. He felt himself dangling as though held suspended by the middle in the fingers of a giant. Then he was aware of the cadence of motion and knew he was draped over the back of a walking horse. His hands were tied and so were his feet, and when he tried to work off the horse's back he found that he was roped to the saddle. Ahead of him sounded the thud of hoofs and he knew that a horseman led the animal on which he was tied. There were no other sounds, but he sensed that they were ascending a path which led into the hills. Presently he lost consciousness again.

Cessation of movement brought him to. He opened his eyes and looked through a lacework of leaves at a canopy of stars. He was lying on his back upon the ground and when he tried to move he found that he was trussed like a roasting fowl. He was sick and utterly helpless.

The leaves rustled under a pair of boots and the dark figure of a man leaned over him. The fellow lifted him, grunting with the effort. Jim tried to speak but his mouth was parched and so swollen that no words came forth. The man bore him on for a dozen feet, dropped him with a growled oath and picking up his feet, dragged him through the brush. Another ten feet and the fellow made an abrupt turn, grinding Jim's shoulders into the gravel. Once more the man bent and Jim felt hands working under his back. There was a heave and he rolled to his right. A rock gouged him in the side, then all pressure was removed.

Too late he realized what had happened, and a cry of fear was wrenched from his bleeding lips. There was nothing under him! He was falling through space!

Down, down he went, still rolling in the air, struggling with the desperation of a doomed man to free his arms and legs. For a seeming eternity he dropped through the black void, then came a jarring shock and blackout.

On the brink above him, a man started pushing dirt into the hole.

CHAPTER FOUR

Once more Jim Randall awoke in a strange bed. The awakening was slow and painful, memory of what had happened finally seeping into a dulled brain to stir him into full consciousness. With the return of his senses came the realization of pressure on his chest.

His eyes snapped open, focusing on a point six inches beneath his chin. It wasn't rock and gravel that weighed him down, it was his own arm encased in a rough board splint. He raised his wondering gaze to the pole rafters overhead and knew that he was lying under a roof; then the sense of smell returned and he became aware of the odor of frying bacon.

Feet stirred and he heard a cheerful voice. "Awake, huh? 'Bout time. By gob, I was thinkin' you'd never come outa it."

He turned his eye to the right and blinked in surprise. The speaker was a little dried-up old man in patched overalls and a faded blue shirt. A bald pate shone above a fringe of straggling gray hair, there was a three days' growth of whiskers on the leathery cheeks and a scraggly moustache tried to hide the man's wide grin. A pair of eyes like bright blue beads danced merrily. It had been a long time since Jim had seen Bill Scott, but he knew him instantly.

"Scotty!" he exclaimed. "What—? How in the world did I get here?"

Bill Scott did not answer him at once. "How you feelin', son?"

"Rotten. Is my arm broken, or did you put this thing on me to hold me down?"

"She's busted, all right. And your leg, too. Not to mention numerous contusions and abrasions, as the *medicos* say."

Jim slanted a glance along the length of his body and saw that his left leg was also in a splint. He looked back at the old prospector. "The last thing I remember I landed with a thud after falling several miles. I also had the impression that somebody was shoveling dirt over me, but that must have been a dream. Where did you find me?"

Scotty shuffled over to the stove, moved the skillet to the back, then returned and lowered himself gently to the edge of the bunk.

"Found you at the bottom of one of my old prospect holes. 'Twasn't no several miles, but she was plenty deep. And that there about the dirt wasn't no dream, neither; you was pretty well covered. How in tarnation didja get in there?"

"I was rolled in. I don't know who did the rolling, but he must have thought I was dead."

"Uh-huh. Well, Providence sure directed me to you. That old glory hole was within a mile of my camp last night, and this mornin' I decided to take a look at her, jest for old time's sake, you might say. I took a right smart of the yaller stuff outa it in its day and there was a sorta sentimental attachment, if you get what I mean. When I got to it I seen right off where somethin' had been drug over the ground and first off I got to wonderin' if somebody'd found some nuggets I'd overlooked; then I seen that the draggin' had been towards the hole instead of away from it. Looked like whatever it was had been drug to the edge of the shaft and then dumped into it.

"Well, I jest hadda see what had been dumped in there, so I knotted some ropes together and slid down. Didn't see nothin' at first but a bunch of gravel, but when I lighted a match by gob if there wasn't a human face stickin' outa it!

"I got down on m'hands and knees and started clawin' at the dirt, and when I got it mostly moved I struck another match. It was you, all wrapped up like an express package. I cut you loose and found your left leg and arm was busted. Reckon you landed on that side, and if you hadn't been tied up so tight the bones woulda come plumb through your hide. Anyhow, I tied you up again, shinnied up the rope and dragged you to the top. Then I loaded you on my Jenny burro and packed you here. That's all."

"That's all," said Jim quietly. "It's plenty. Scotty, I reckon you saved my bacon and no mistake."

"And why shouldn't I?" demanded Scotty vehemently. "Just about every time I needed a outfit your daddy grubstaked me. Time and time again he done it, and never would he take a note or a written agreement between us. I tell you, Providence directed me there and I'd got you out if I hadda claw my way to the top with you on my back. Ain't a better man livin' or dead than John Randall, and when they said he'd robbed the bank and blowed his brains out I told 'em they was a pack of ijits! I don't care what it looked like; a burn on the head don't mean a man shot hisself, and as to the missin' money—well, mebbe figgers don't lie but liars sure as hell can figger!"

Jim reached out with his good hand and gripped the old fellow by the knee. His face was set and grim. "You're right, Scotty; right as rain! That's why you found me in that shaft. Whoever killed my father has been trying ever since I left Montana to kill me because they knew I wouldn't swallow that story any more than you have."

"So that's why you was in that hole! They been tryin' to kill you!"

Jim explained to the old prospector what had happened on his trip south and since then, and Scotty listened with his little blue eyes wide and his seamed face alive with interest.

"Looky here," he said. "I betcha my Jenny against a box of burned matches that somebody killed John Randall figgerin' to get hold of the Star and a bunch of cash to boot. Betcha he cleaned out the bank and then shot John to make it look like he done it. Then he bought the Star with the money he stole and—"

"Whoa!" interrupted Jim. "I've thought that all over and there's lots of objections to it. First off, Dad acknowledged a shortage of fifty thousand dollars when he signed that mortgage. And he did sign it. Brent Wood witnessed his signature and Brent's four-square. The other twenty thousand shortage occurred after the first audit had been made. Whoever did it might have taken that twenty thousand knowing that its theft would be blamed on Dad, but it wouldn't be enough to buy the Star."

"Nope; but it would make the Star cost him only thirty thousand instead of fifty. Lots of fellers been murdered for less'n twenty thousand dollars. Jim, who do you think done it?"

"I wish I knew. The best guess is that it was somebody connected with the bank. There were three there besides Dad: Lew Dunham, Brent Wood and Jason Rudd, the bookkeeper."

"If it's one of them three I reckon you don't need three guesses. I never did cotton to Lew Dunham; he got a face like a Labrador iceberg and a handshake like a deceased cod. But he's smart; you'll sure have a job on your hands gettin' the goods on that jasper."

"I know it. There's not a bit of proof and the trail's mighty cold." He lay for a moment staring at the rafters above; then, "How long do you figure I'll be laid up here?"

"Well, you got sundry bruises and contusions and a bad shakin' up, but outside of that busted leg and arm they ain't much to worry about. You're gonna have to dress and eat one-handed for a spell and it's a cinch you ain't to do much walkin' for a month or six weeks.

Jim groaned. "And meanwhile—"

"Meanwhile what? Ain't nothin' Lew Dunham can do that he ain't done already, is they?"

"No; but lying here helpless, knowing that people think my father was a thief, a suicide—!"

"Let 'em think it. Let 'em waller in the knowledge. Then when you prove that he didn't clean out the bank and didn't shoot his-self mebbe some of 'em as needs religion will get it. Looky here, Jim, just what are you fixin' to do first?"

"I've got to find out who's behind the Acme Cattle Company. Maybe the killer had nothing to do with the company, but I've got to know for sure."

"Folks say it's some Eastern outfit."

"That's right. If I can find the city I can get a detective agency or the Chief of Police to find out about them for me. That'll take time, and I can't make a move until I know."

"You ain't gonna make a move for some time whether you know or not," said Scotty. "But the feller that buried you in that hole thinks you're dead, and—Hey! Mebbe layin' low and playin' dead for a spell might be a pretty good idee! The killer might get careless, figgerin' you're safe under the sod, and tip off his hand!"

Jim's eyes brightened. "Scotty, I think you got something there! But if I'm lying here, how am I going to know if he does tip off his hand?"

"By gob, I'll know!" Scotty was even more enthusiastic than was Jim. "Lissen! I'll hike down to Briscoe and keep watch for you! I got me a little grubstake and lots of time on my hands."

Jim was doubtful. "Think you can do any good?"

"You leave that to me, son! I'll hang around the saloons and get drunk and let people stumble over me and cuss me for bein' in the way, and all the time I'll have one eye and both ears open. You'd be surprised what you can pick up playin' drunk."

"Scotty, will you?"

"Will a fish swim? You jest watch me!"

For a few seconds young man and oldster exchanged hope-ful, expectant glances; then Scotty got up and went quickly over to the stove.

"First off we got to eat. Or I do. You can't eat. You're dead."

Linda Lane came out of the Star ranch house and paused on the gallery to draw on her gloves. Waiting at the steps with two horses was Jeff Dirk, his eyes glowing at the sight of her. She felt his intent gaze and glanced at him curiously.

He said softly, "Linda, you're the most beautiful thing alive!"

"Thank you, kind sir; although I'm sure you don't really mean it."

"But I do mean it!"

"And me with a sunblistered nose and a whole flock of new freckles!"

"I love every one of 'em!" he declared ardently.

She came down to where he stood and he held her stirrup while she mounted, then vaulted into his own saddle.

"In just two months," she said as they moved across the range, "I've come to feel like a dyed-in-the-wool Westerner. I've learned to ride—I *do* ride fairly well, don't I, Jeff?"

"You sit that hull like a regular cowhand."

"And I'm learning to rope and shoot. And please don't tell me that I handle a gun like Annie Oakley."

"You're right good at hitting a stationary target."

"I suppose so; but I'd like to shoot like you and Panhandle— just whip out the gun and let fly without aiming. It looks so easy, but I've practiced and practiced and it takes ages to get my gun out of the holster. And then I generally miss."

"You've practiced just about two weeks; Panhandle and I have been at it all our lives. There's a difference. And you don't need a fast draw. We do. Our lives may depend upon our speed some day."

"Yes." She sobered at a memory. "I'll never forget that night at the Junction. I've never told you about it, have I? It was when father and I were on our way here; we stopped over at the Junction and got rooms at the hotel. In the middle of the night I heard shots and ran to my door. A man came out of the room opposite mine. He had a gun in his hand and a bullet smashed the panel of his door just as he closed it.

"He turned and I saw his face; it was hard and set, with little wrinkles at the corners of his eyes. Then I heard a shot from down the hall and he leaped sideways and I saw him stagger as the bullet hit him. His gun whipped up and I could see it jump in his hand as he fired. He didn't cock it—just held the trigger back and worked the hammer with his thumb. I guess I screamed, for he turned towards me, took two stumbling steps and fell at my feet."

"Enter, the hero," said Dirk. "Tall and handsome and with curly brown hair."

"How did you know it was Jim Randall?"

He gave a start. "Randall?"

"Yes. I never saw such fast shooting. He killed the man at the head of the stairs, shot him through the lungs three times. And he was wounded when he did it; he just shot by instinct."

"I guess the fellow can shoot," admitted Dirk grudgingly, remembering the battle which had ended so disastrously for his men.

Linda looked towards Jim's homestead. "I wonder where he is now."

"Still running, I guess. That notice we found on the table in his cabin sure brought out the yellow in him."

She turned to him indignantly. "It did no such thing! I don't care what else you say about Jim Randall, you can't call him a coward."

"So you're defending him, huh? What's he to you, anyhow?"

"Nothing. Nothing but a memory." There was a faraway look in her eyes. "A memory of courage and grit and loyalty. That day in the store when we heard him defend his father and swear to run down the story he'd heard about him—I thought that was fine. No, Jeff, he hasn't run away; he's just busy running down that story about his father and he'll be back."

"Want to bet?"

"Yes!"

"All right. How's this for a wager: If Jim Randall doesn't show up within a month you marry me; if he does, I'll step out of the picture in favor of Jason Rudd—or Randall himself."

It was his first attempt at boldness and for a moment Linda simply stared at him. "Just like that," she said. "The question of love has nothing to do with it. You'd gamble with marriage just as you would with a horse."

"I'm not gambling. I know Randall won't come back."

"If you're so sure, you must know what became of him!"

The accusation was unexpected and he covered his discomfiture with a show of anger. "Of course I know what became of him. He's dragged his stake, I tell you. I know the man, know he's yellow at the core. His father shot himself because he couldn't face the music. And he shot himself in Briscoe. If Randall wanted to run down the story he'd do it right here."

She did not answer him, and for a short space they walked their horses in silence; but he saw that her chin was in the air and knew by the set of her face that she had been deeply stirred. Presently he reached out and took her hand. "Aw, honey, forget it," he begged. "Jim Randall's all right; I just see red when you show an interest in anybody else. Jason Rudd, for instance. It seems to me he's always at the house. And he rarely calls without bringing you some sort of present. Flowers—candy—a new riding quirt!"

Linda answered calmly. "Jason comes over to see father; they like to play checkers and I think they're cooking up some kind of business deal."

"Yeah? What kind of deal?"

"I don't know, and I wouldn't tell if I did without their permission. Look, Jeff! There's smoke coming from the chimney of Jim's place! And horses in the corral! I've won my bet!"

"Not by a long shot. They're Box D horses. Lew Dunham's taken over the place. Asked me if the Star had any objection; said he'd like to winter some cattle there."

"But that's Jim's place; Dunham can't do that."

"He figures Jim isn't coming back."

They turned their horses into the Briscoe trail and put them to a lope. The wind of their passage kissed Linda's cheeks and whipped at the curls which gleamed beneath the brim of her Stetson; her eyes were bright and eager. Always the surge of power in the animal she rode, the swift rush through the clean air, exhilarated her. She found herself wishing that she were alone.

For, if the truth is to be told, Dirk's constant attendance upon her was becoming a bit irksome. He was handsome and pictur-esque, the cowboy ideal of the Easterner, and at first she had been fascinated. Now she had learned to look beneath the surface, to search for qualities other than smartness of dress and deftness of conversation, and had found them lacking in Dirk. When she had seen Jim Randall he was dusty and dishevelled and bleeding, but the steadfast fire in his soul had shone through the grime and she had instinctively known him to be a real man.

They went into the hotel lobby together and found there Alonzo Lane, Lew Dunham and Jason Rudd. The three were in chairs drawn closely together and were talking in low, earnest tones. Jason got up quickly, his face beaming, and came over to greet Linda. "Good morning, Miss Lane. Are you staying for dinner?"

She told him that she was, that she was tired of her own cook-ing and since her father had had to come to town she decided she might as well ride in.

"You will be my guest," insisted Rudd. "The—ah—enterprize entered into by your father and myself is about to be concluded. I'll have some interesting news for you. Suppose I engage a room so that you can rest a bit before dinner?"

"That would be nice of you," Linda said, and Jeff Dirk, who had been completely ignored, swore under his breath and stamped out of the lobby. This insignificant little bookkeeper was always getting the jump on him. Why hadn't he thought of getting a room for Linda? He crossed to the nearest saloon in search of liquid consolation.

When Linda came downstairs she found Rudd waiting for her. His black suit was a bit worn and shiny but his linen was immaculate and his ruddy little face shone behind the thick-lensed glasses. Linda smiled inwardly; he was a nice little man, but how in the world could Jeff imagine that she was romantically interested in him?

Lane and Dunham had already gone into the diningroom, and Jason and Linda followed. There was a long table with benches upon which sat the ordinary customers, and two smaller tables reserved for special guests. One of these was occupied by her father and Lew Dunham; to the other one she was escorted by the beaming Rudd. As she seated herself a withered old prospector lurched into the room and took a place on the bench at the long table directly behind her. He looked around at her and croaked, "Howdy, Miss Linda."

She gave him a smile and a pleasant, "Hello, Scotty," and explained to Rudd, "Scotty is one of my particular friends. I found him camped on our range once and had dinner with him. The yarns he tells are taller than the com of Iowa. But, Jason—that news you promised me?"

"Ah, yes; the news. Well, Miss Lane, tomorrow afternoon the Miners and Merchants Bank of Briscoe will re-open. The officers will be yours truly, cashier and bookkeeper; Lewis Dunham, vice-president; and Alonzo Lane, president."

"How wonderful!" she cried. "It's what father has always wanted. Mr. Rudd, how did you manage it?"

Jason made a deprecating gesture. "I suggested it to your father that first day I called. Like him, I enjoy that kind of work, but of course I hadn't the means to handle such a big undertaking alone. He succeeded in interesting the Acme people and they are furnishing the necessary capital. I believe we'll make a success of it."

"I'm sure you will! Just to think of it—father the president of a real honest-to-goodness bank!"

"Sh-h-h-h!" warned Jason, smiling. "I don't suppose there's any harm in letting it be known, but I'd rather have the others announce it. After all, I'm just the bookkeeper."

Thereafter they talked in lower tones, lingering over their dinner. Long before they had finished, Scotty had risen from his bench and shuffled through the doorway. Linda finally left the three men to continue their conference and went outside to find Jeff Dirk waiting for her. He was a bit surly as he helped her into the saddle and for a while they rode side by side without speaking.

"I didn't see you at dinner," Linda finally said. "Don't tell me your appetite has failed you."

"Had a bite at the Chink restaurant. I didn't want my dinner spoiled by seeing Jason Rudd grinning at you."

For the second time that day he rubbed the fur the wrong way. "Jeff," she said quietly, "I think it's time we had an understanding, don't you? We've been very good friends and I appreciate the interest you've shown in me, but surely you can't say that I've given you any reason to believe that my liking for you is any deeper than that of a good friend."

Jeff made a fierce gesture. "That's the hell of it. I'm crazy about you and have been ever since the first day I saw you, but you haven't said a word that would make me think that you look on me as anything more than a brother. And, damn it, I don't want to be a brother."

"Then please don't act like one. Brothers and sisters, you know, are supposed to quarrel. I like you, Jeff, really I do; but you aren't entitled to act like a jealous lover and when you do it certainly doesn't increase my regard for you."

"I know. I'll try to watch my step. But Jason Rudd—"

She interrupted firmly. "Jason Rudd has been a good friend to father and me. He's made it possible for father to enter the field he's always liked. Jeff, I'm going to tell you a secret. The Briscoe bank is going to re-open."

"What?" So surprised was Dirk that he jerked his horse to a halt.

"Yes. Tomorrow. Mr. Rudd will be bookkeeper and cashier, Mr. Dunham vice-president, and father will be president. Isn't it wonderful?"

He stared at her for a moment, then automatically said "Yeah." The word seemed wrung from him. Realizing that she was looking puzzledly at him, he urged his horse to a walk and they resumed their way.

"Yes," he repeated, "that's great." But there was no enthusiasm in his voice.

CHAPTER FIVE

J IM RANDALL was about to turn in when he heard the pat-
ter of burro hoofs and a moment later the voice of Scotty as
he talked to the little animal while stripping him. Jim lighted
the lamp and when Scotty entered he knew by the old fellow's
expression that he was the bearer of news.

"Something at last?" he asked eagerly.

"Nothin' about the Acme. Same old story—no comp'ny of
that name listed in the Philadelphy directory and nobody that
ever heard of it. By god, I heard Lane say to that bookkeeper feller
that he had got word from the Acme in Philadelphy, and Harry
Finch, the stage agent that give the telegram to Lane, told me it
was from Philadelphy; yet when I sent a wire to that same Acme
Cattle Comp'y in Philadelphy it came back undelivered. By gob,
it got me stopped."

Jim sat down on the edge of the bunk. "Funny that neither
the Chief of Police or that detective firm we hired can dig them
up. Looks as though we're bucking a smart outfit, Scotty. They
just don't want to be found."

Scotty tamped some tobacco in his corncob pipe and put a
match to it. "You know, this thing's jest like a spring—the more
you stir it, the muddier it gets. But here's the news I rode out to
give you: the Miners and Merchants Bank of Briscoe is goin' to
re-open its doors tomorrow."

Jim stared at him. "Who's opening it?"

"The Acme's puttin' up the *dinero*. Alonzo Lane, president; Lew
Dunham, vice-president; Jason Rudd, bookkeeper and cashier."

"Nothing in that to get excited about, is there? The bank was bound to re-open some day."

Scotty puffed thoughtfully for a while. "Depends," he said at last. "You and me got the hunch that in some way somebody got away with seventy thousand dollars and made your father the goat. His'try repeats itself, they say. The bank's been reorganized and the feller we got our eyes on is back in the saddle as vice-president; how do we know that he ain't shapin' things up to get another big chunk of dough at somebody's expense?"

"I get it. This time it'll be Lane who's the goat."

"I dunno. Lane was sent out by the Acme, wherever they are. Seems to me like that bookkeeper feller would make a good goat this time."

Jim thought it over for a moment. "Scotty, it would be mighty risky to try the same stunt twice. Folks might swallow one looting and one suicide, but I don't think they'd stand for two."

"Don't have to be a second suicide. Mebbe the feller aims to make this a final clean-up and get out. If it was Dunham, he could sell out on the quiet, get all set to pull stakes, and then, when everything was right, clean out the bank and get out."

"That's right. If Lew Dunham is behind the Acme, he could pretend to sell his ranch to that outfit and run both the Star and the Box D at a distance. Scotty, you may have something there. How did you learn about the bank?"

"Took a seat in the hotel dinin' room right near Linda Lane and Jason Rudd. I heard him tell her and she was tickled pink. Said that's what her daddy always wanted, to be president of a bank. Say, it's a danged shame she's tangled up with that outfit. She's a mighty fine gal. Jason just sets and glows when he's with her, and you can't blame him. Anyhow, he looked like Solomon in all his glory. Jeff Dirk fetched her to town and Rudd grabs her off for dinner, which same didn't please Jeff none a-tall, you can bet your old sombrero."

Jim's face tightened a bit. Strange, he told himself, that he should resent the attention of other men to Linda Lane. None of his business at all; but he always must remember her as she stood at the doorway with her hands at her throat, and later when she knelt by his bed and gave him the courage to suffer with a smile.

"Well," said Scotty, "what are we goin' to do about it?"

"About what? Oh!" Jim pulled his thoughts back to the present. "The only thing we can do is keep digging and hoping. I think I'll go back to the homestead tomorrow. I got a fence to build and cattle to round up. They're scattered all over the range. No use playing dead any longer."

"How's the leg?"

"I can use it. The arm's nearly as good as new. I've been exercising it regularly. Panhandle and his pals still around?"

"Yep. Baskin' in the smiles of the populace. Everybody seems to know about their jumpin' you, and thinks they scared you out of the country. They sure will be surprised when you show up."

"The one who kicked me into that shaft was Panhandle; I heard him cuss. Scotty, if I could get the drop on him some time in a place where we wouldn't be interrupted I might be able to make him talk."

"I doubt if he can tell you any more than who pays him, and you can take it from me that won't be the gent behind the deal. He's too foxy to leave any loose ends. And say! Did I tell you that Lew Dunham moved a couple fellers and a bunch of yearlin's over on your place?"

"No, you didn't. He can move them right back again."

"Keno. I'll mosey along back there with you."

"I don't think you better had, Scotty. I don't want you to get too friendly with me. You keep on hanging around Briscoe and pass on to me what you pick up. Now let's go to bed."

Early the following morning Jim rode out of the hills behind his cabin and drew rein before an astonished Box D cowboy. "Howdy, Jake," he said.

"Jim Randall! What in time you doin' here? I thought—"

"Thought that I didn't live here anymore? You're wrong, Jake. This is my home. What are *you* doing here?"

"Why—why, Lew sent me over. Me and Digger. He sorta figured that you—Say, you ain't come back to stay, have you?"

"You guessed it. Suppose you round up Digger and start those Box D cows moving back to their home ranch, huh? I want this grass for my own stock."

"Sure, Jim. Sure, I'll find him." Still wondering, he went to the corral for his horse. Jim went into the cabin and saw him through the window as he rode away. The two men, he noticed, had kept the place clean. Presently Jake returned with Digger and they started to bunch the yearlings. Jake stopped at the cabin before they left. "We'll be back for our bedrolls," he told Jim. "We'll have our hands full gittin' these critters off this good range."

When they returned a couple hours later Lew Dunham was with them. Jim went outside to meet him and his two cowboys entered the cabin to get their belongings.

"So you came back," said Lew, his cold eyes on Randall. "Some folks are just too dumb to know when they're licked."

"Nobody likes to be called dumb, Lew, even if they are. Call me stubborn. I just can't seem to let go something that belongs to me."

"What happened to you?"

"You wouldn't know, would you, Lew?"

"No, I wouldn't know."

"Well, a bunch jumped me back there in the shed. They beat me up and made a Christmas package of me and carried me up into the hills. One of them tossed me into an old mine shaft like a dead cat and shoveled dirt on me. But he didn't make a very good job of it and I'm stubborn. I came back."

"Take you more'n a month to make the trip?"

"I had a broken arm and some bad bruises. I found a prospector's cabin and a cache of supplies. I'm as good as new now, and they don't catch me napping again."

"You're not only stubborn, you're foolish. The next time they'll make sure the cat's dead before they bury it. Jim, your best bet is to sell out to me."

"Too stubborn," sighed Jim. "And always hoping there won't be a next time."

The two cowboys came out of the cabin, and Lew rode away with them.

Jim rode to Briscoe around noon and learned that the bank opening ceremonies were scheduled for one o'clock. The astonishment of the townspeople at sight of him was amusing; they stared as though he had risen from the dead, which, figuratively, he had. He saw Scotty in town, apparently three sheets in the wind. This too Jim found amusing; Scotty could absorb enough liquor to float a battleship without showing it.

He was entering the hotel when he met Linda Lane and Jeff Dirk coming out. They stopped short at sight of him, and Linda, with a little exclamation, came hurrying to him. "Jim! You *did* come back! Oh, I knew you would!" She gave him her hand, then flashed a triumphant glance at the frowning Dirk. "We had a little bet on it; remember, Jeff?"

"You didn't take me up," said Dirk stiffly. "Come on; we'd better be getting down to the bank. Your father's going to make a speech."

"Of course. Jim, they've re-opened the bank and made father president. Do come down and hear him speak; and when you get a chance, drop in to see us, won't you?"

Jim smiled at her and stepped to one side to let them pass. His heart was thumping. Her attitude towards him had changed; there had been genuine gladness in her greeting and she had even asked him to call. The world seemed suddenly brighter.

A cloud appeared in the shape of Panhandle. He was riding along the street and happened to turn his head and see Randall. Astonishment caused him to jerk his horse to an abrupt halt, and for the space of five heartbeats he sat staring. And Jim, for all his dislike of the man, grinned at him. There was no mirth in the grin and his eyes were hard, and Panhandle knew that Randall had recognized him that night and had returned to get him. He urged his horse on with his knees, his gaze still on Jim, the fingers of his right hand gripping the gun butt at his side. When he was out of sight he swore harshly. "I got to get him first," he told himself. "I just got to!"

He turned into an alley and tied behind a shed in the back of Joe's Place, scanned his surroundings carefully before venturing into the open, then entered the saloon by its rear door. A quick glance reassured him except for a single bartender he was alone. He bought a bottle of whiskey and retired to a table in the darkest corner. "I buried him," he mumbled. "Dumped him into that shaft and covered him. He can't be alive!"

But he couldn't deny the evidence of his own eyes; Jim Randall was alive and the probability was that Jim Randall had returned to get him. He gulped another drink and then a third. Why not have it done and over with? Randall had killed his brother and his brother's blood cried for vengeance. He had openly boasted that he would kill Randall. The man wasn't bulletproof; a slug through the heart—

He downed another drink and went over to the doorway. A crowd had gathered before the bank and somebody was making a speech. Seated on a watering trough on the fringe of the crowd was Jim Randall. Panhandle sized up the situation and made his plan. He went back into the alley, crouched, whipped out his gun and drew the hammer in one swift motion. For a few seconds he held the weapon level, then gently lowered the hammer and holstered the gun. He was not satisfied; it was too slow; he was out of practice.

He drew again. Better but still not fast enough. Three more times he went through the motions of drawing the gun and pulling the hammer back with taut thumb while the forefinger held the trigger, then with a nod of satisfaction he holstered the Colt and started along the alley on foot. He'd come upon Randall from the rear, call him an insulting name and shoot him as he turned.

When he reached the end of the alley he crossed to the one on the far side of the street and followed it to a point where he could reach the sidewalk some fifty feet from where Randall was seated. Passing between two buildings he halted at a front corner to reconnoiter. The crowd was still gathered before the bank and he could hear the voice of Alonzo Lane. Randall still sat on the watering trough. Sprawled on the steps of a store between Panhandle and Randall was Bill Scott, hat drawn over his eyes, apparently drunk.

Panhandle started along the sidewalk, his gaze on Randall, a hand ready to snatch out his gun. Forty feet, thirty. He passed Scotty without a glance. Twenty feet. Another five would make a sure thing of it.

"Hey, Panhandle!"

Scotty's shrill voice rose above that of Alonzo Lane and the heads of the audience turned as though they were one. Jim leaped to his feet, wheeling. Panhandle cursed and yanked his gun. There was no time to provoke Jim into drawing first, he must get him right now. His Colt was out and levelled before the surprised Jim could get his weapon clear. Panhandle thumbed the hammer and heard instead of the booming report a futile click of metal on metal.

He realized in a flash why the gun had missed fire. He kept five cartridges in the cylinder, with the sixth space unloaded under the hammer. Back of Joe's Place he had taken five practice draws, and each time he had pulled the hammer and lowered it again the cylinder had revolved one notch. This, the sixth, had thrown the empty chamber into firing position.

All this in a single instant, and in the same split second he knew that his carelessness had cost him his life. There was no time for a second shot; Jim's weapon spat flame and lead and

Panhandle rocked back on his heels and then fell forward with his face in the dust.

Jim ran quickly to him, the crowd following. Kneeling, Jim rolled the man to his back. "Panhandle!" he said sharply. "Snap out of it! Who was it that hired you to get me? Tell me, man; *who was it?*"

Panhandle's eyes flickered open and in them Randall read unutterable hate. His lips moved and Jim caught the first two words of a three-word sentence. "Go—to—!"

Then Panhandle proceeded to go there himself.

Jeb Mosley, the town marshal, came shouldering through the crowd. He said, "What's goin' on here, Randall?"

Dirk and Linda had followed him and Dirk said, "It's plain enough, isn't it? Randall shot him; drew on him before he had a chance." His voice was thick with rage.

"By gob, that ain't so!" blazed old Scotty. "I was settin' on the steps and seen the whole show. Panhandle aimed to get Jim as he turned and would have if his gun hadn't failed."

"How about it?" asked the marshal, sweeping the crowd with a glance. "Any of you folks see it?"

Several of them nodded. "Mr. Scott's right," came Linda's clear voice. "I heard them shout and turned just in time to see it."

"Well, if that's the way of it—"

"It is." Jim got to his feet. "Panhandle's been after my scalp. He tried to kill me at Cottonwood Junction and several times since."

"Why'd he want to kill you?"

"To earn a nice little bonus from somebody."

The marshal frowned. "That's puttin' it right strong, Randall. Who'd hire him to do a thing like that?"

"If I knew, I wouldn't have wasted my lead on him."

Mosley indicated two men who stood near him. "You, Will and Sandy, get a shutter and tote him down to Benson's. I'll follow directly." They moved away and he came over to Jim and spoke in a low voice. "If I was you, Randall, I'd sell out and hit the trail. If somebody's out to get you he'll not stop now. Better drift while your health's good." He nodded to add emphasis to his advice and moved on down the street.

The crowd broke up, many of them going into the bank. Jim turned and he saw Jeff Dirk talking with Lew Dunham, leaving Linda alone for the moment. He walked over to her and spoke quietly. "Thanks for putting in a good word for me, Miss Linda. I'm afraid Jeff Dirk won't like what you did."

"I can't help that," she said shortly. "Jeff was mistaken. But was it necessary to kill the man?"

"I didn't have any choice. Maybe it won't seem so bad if I tell you that he was the one was shot at me through the window that night at the Junction."

"Oh!" Her eyes went wide. "And he worked for the Star!"

"He probably got a job with the Star just for an excuse for hanging around Briscoe. He really worked for somebody who wants me out of circulation; someone who's afraid I'll find out the truth about my father's death."

"You still don't believe that John Randall robbed the bank?"

"I never have believed it. Or that he committed suicide. If you knew my father you wouldn't believe it either." He saw Dirk approaching and turned away.

He ate dinner at the Chinese restaurant, bought some necessary supplies which he put in a gunnysack and tied behind his saddle, and started for home. He had accounted for one of his enemies and regretted it slightly. Panhandle was a connecting link; through him he might have learned at least the name of his employer. Now that connecting link was gone. From where he stood it looked as though Jeff Dirk were an intermediary of some kind, with Lew Dunham at the top or near it; but thus far he had no more to back his theory than a hunch.

That theory was logical enough. Simply stated it was that Lew Dunham had looted the bank, blamed the theft on Jim's father, then killed him in such a way as to make it appear that he had committed suicide. With the money he had stolen, he bought the Star, using a fictitious Eastern company to cover the deal. Fearing that Jim might return unexpectedly and investigate, Lew had written him and then had set Panhandle on his trail to kill him before he reached Briscoe. Now that the bank had been re-opened, Lew would quietly "sell" his ranch to the Acme and at the proper time loot the bank and vanish. As the mysterious Acme Cattle Company he could still collect the profits from both ranches, leaving Dirk in charge as a reward for services rendered. Or, if he wished, he could sell both ranches.

It made sense except for two things. First, if Dunham was as smart as Jim thought him, he would not permit Dirk to know or suspect the truth for fear that the man would forever hold it over him; and, second, John Randall had acknowledged a debt of fifty thousand dollars by executing a mortgage against the Star for that amount. Jim got the mortgage and cancelled note from the lining of his coat and examined the signatures again. They were undoubtedly genuine.

"If only he had left some word," muttered Jim. "Some explanation or record of his deals." But, he told himself in the next instant, if John Randall had left such a record, the guilty one would have certainly destroyed it. Unless it had been overlooked. He had searched the bank without success, but there remained his father's office in the ranch house. If only he could get into that office for half an hour!

He thought it over as he rode towards the homestead, and the more he considered the more convinced he became that the ranch house was the place to search. Getting inside would be no problem to him; the results of the search might well prove worth the risk.

It was close to two in the morning when he sighted the Star buildings. The big house stood silver in the moonlight and a deep silence hung over it. No light showed and Jim knew that behind its walls Linda Lane and her father slept in the bedrooms in the wing he was approaching. The office was in the near front corner, adjoining the livingroom, and in the far wing were dining room and kitchen. Bunkhouse and mess shack were located on the far side of the house.

Jim halted at a safe distance, dismounted and tied, then removed his spurs and moved silently towards the building. Presently he circled to avoid passing the bedrooms, still keeping the house between him and the crew's quarters. Occasionally he stopped to listen and gaze about him.

He reached the long gallery at last, softly mounted it and tried the front door. It was barred. Moving to a window, he felt for a moment with his fingers then inserted the blade of his knife in the crack which had been there since he was a boy. He slipped the catch and gently raised the sash. He listened for a few seconds, then climbed noiselessly inside. He was in the gloom now, but the doorway to the office stood out clear against the moonlight which streamed through the window of the little room. Silently he stole through the doorway and into the office.

The place was just as his father had left it, with the rolltop desk in a corner, left side towards the east window. He went to it, moved the big chair to one side and began going through the drawers. One by one he emptied them of their contents, carefully returning each article to its place as he finished examining it. And almost at once he came upon a letter from a lawyer in Philadelphia. He struck a match and by its brief flare read the address, which he memorized. At least he had found a clue to the ownership of the Acme: through this lawyer he might be able to locate the firm....

Outside, on the top of the ridge which paralleled the hills, a horseman halted, his gaze on the Box D ranch house. He had caught sight of a momentary glow beyond one of the windows and was trying to fathom the meaning of it.

For several minutes he remained there, as motionless as an Indian scout, then he spoke softly to his horse and moved down the slope, gaze still fixed on the window near the front. Suddenly it appeared again, a dim glow which shone briefly then died. The horseman angled off towards the northwest, swung to the ground and led the horse to the corral. Here Jeff Dirk tied the animal, then walked cautiously towards the house....

Examination of the desk drawers having failed to uncover anything belonging to his father, Jim tackled the pigeonholes. Slowly and methodically he went about it, occasionally flicking a match into life to aid identification. There was nothing, and the conviction finally reached him that the authorities must have searched the house also.

He stood before the desk for a short while, thinking. Where else could his father have put such records as he kept? Slowly he turned, struck another match and gazed about the room. A rag rug, woven by his mother; a chair; a small stand with a lamp on it; on the wall a mounted elkhead and pegs upon which John Randall hung his hat and coat; and a cabinet in which were kept remedies for man and beast.

His gaze remained on the cabinet, his forehead wrinkled in concentration. A boyhood picture slowly formed in his mind. It was the day he had ridden the wild, unbroken horse they had called Outlaw. He had ridden him to a standstill and had burst into his father's office to tell of his achievement. John Randall was standing before that cabinet and young Jim had noticed that it had been swung out from its place on hinges and stood at a right angle to the wall. At the time he had thought little of this, his mind occupied with the news he had brought his father; only now did the significance of the moving cabinet reach him.

He crossed the floor to the cabinet, grasped and pulled. It did not budge. Striking another match, Jim examined it carefully, noticed the strip of wood which ran up one side. He pressed this and felt it give under his fingers, and now when he pulled the cabinet swung outward.

There was a black opening behind it and into this he thrust his hand. There was a single object in there and he drew it out. There was not light enough to see it plainly, but he knew it was a tally book. Then he heard a sound in the room outside, the noise of a boot scraping on wood. He swung the cabinet shut, book clutched in his hands. In two swift strides he was at the door. There was a man in the act of climbing through the window through which Jim had entered.

The man called sharply, "Hold it, you!" but his hands were engaged and he was not in position to draw his gun immediately.

Jim glanced quickly over his shoulder and saw the head and shoulders of another man outside the office window. Escape by that means was barred to him. He sprang through the doorway into the livingroom and turned sharply to his right and into the corridor leading to the bedrooms. At the end of that corridor was a door opening on the patio. He started along the hall and stopped abruptly as the nearest bedroom door opened. The moonlight which flowed through the bedroom window outlined the form of Linda Lane, and she stood much as she had stood that other night he remembered so well.

She spoke sharply. "Who are you? What do you want?"

The Star crew was no longer silent; he could hear voices at the front of the house and knew that it would be only a matter of seconds before the man in the window admitted them. He answered swiftly. "Jim Randall. Linda, keep this for me. Keep it safe. It's mine; my father's." He thrust the book into the hand which she involuntarily extended.

"Where did you get it?" Her voice was low but intense.

"From a hiding place where he put it. Believe me, Linda! Everything I'm trying to do to prove his innocence may hang on your keeping it for me."

Men were coming into the house and Jim could hear the questions they flung at the one who had admitted them. Jim said, "Get inside—quick!" and as she closed the door he turned and ran along the hall. He found the door to the patio, opened it and looked out. Behind him a gun roared and he heard the sing of lead. He couldn't hesitate any longer. Leaping through the doorway he ran swiftly and silently towards the end of the wing, then stopped abruptly as a man rounded the corner. The fellow halted also and whipped up his gun. In the moonlight he could not be sure of Jim's identity. "Who are you?" he snapped.

Jim leaped at him, seized him by the wrist as he fired. The man let the gun drop and circled Jim with both arms and they went down together. Randall gripped him by the hair, thumped his head on the ground. The fellow let out a yell and struck Jim in the face. Once more Randall crashed his head against the ground and this time the Star puncher went limp.

Jim got to his feet in time to meet two more of them. Others were behind him; he could hear the pound of their boots. He felled one with a rocklike right to the jaw, but before he could strike out again the fellow's companion was on him. And then the men from behind came running up and Jim knew with a feeling of despair that he could not hope to escape.

They dragged him down, held him powerless while his hands were roped behind him; then they jerked him to his feet and held him. Jeff Dirk came up and leaned forward, peering into his face.

"You, huh?" he grunted. "Might have known it. Well, Mister Randall, I guess this cooks your goose. This is burglary and you'll do a couple years in the pen as sure as you're a foot high."

CHAPTER SIX

THE MAN Jim had knocked out pushed himself erect, got to his feet and glared at Jim, "If I had my way I know what I'd do," he growled. "I'd hang the skunk by the neck until dead."

The suggestion appealed to Jeff Dirk, but for obvious reasons he vetoed it. His suit with Linda was not prospering and such an action would surely terminate whatever chance he stood of winning her. To brand Jim as a criminal, to send him to prison, was much better.

"Nothing doing," he said coldly. "We'll lock him in the woodshed for the rest of the night and I'll watch him myself."

So Jim was pushed over to the leanto behind the kitchen and escorted through the doorway by four of them. Here he was quickly searched by the light of a lantern and his knife and gun and what money he had in his pockets were taken from him. Fortunately, they missed the papers in the lining of his coat and also the money belt he wore beneath his clothes.

The outside door was stout but had no lock; so Jeff ordered two of them to get a length of four-by-four timber which was then propped against it. A stake driven into the ground held the timber securely at one end and a spike in the door prevented it from slipping at the other. This done, Dirk went into the ranch house kitchen and thence into the woodshed to inspect the prison.

Like the house the woodshed was of logs, with a heavy board roof topped with sod. There were no windows, and after an ax and a saw had been removed nothing remained which could be used to dig into the hard packed dirt floor but lengths of firewood. With his hands tied behind him Jim was as secure as he would have been in the Briscoe jail.

Jeff called the men out and closed the door which led into the kitchen. There was a bar to this and he fastened it in place. "You can turn in," he told the crew. "I'll plant myself here in the kitchen where I can hear him if he tries any shenanigans."

Alonzo Lane, hastily dressed, joined Dirk in the kitchen. He said, "I looked around pretty thoroughly and can't find a thing missing."

"He didn't have time to get away with anything," said Dirk. "But breaking and entering is enough to send him up for quite a stretch. He forced one of the gallery windows."

Lane went back to bed, pausing at his daughter's bedroom to tell her that Randall had been caught and describing how securely he had been penned in the leanto. "He won't get away; not with Jeff on guard," he concluded.

In the kitchen Dirk drew a chair up to the table and pulled a mail-order catalog over to him, prepared to finish out a sleepless night. He was feeling pretty good about the way things were going. Just that night he had had a meeting with his boss and had been told that he must devise some sure way of getting rid of Randall. All the boss wanted was Randall's removal from that part of the country until certain plans had matured. And Dirk, pondering the matter and seeking a way to carry out the order, had arrived at the Star in time to catch the fellow where he wanted him.

In the woodshed Jim Randall sat disconsolately on a stack of wood. The lantern had been left burning and by its light he saw that escape without aid was just about impossible, even if he had his hands to work with. He knew from the sounds how they had secured the door, and the thick logs presented a barrier as impenetrable as steel.

On the morrow they would take him to the county seat and formally charge him with breaking and entering, and he had no defense except the rather lame excuse that he was searching for his father's effects. He held a court order which would make stealthy entry unnecessary, and he couldn't mention the tally book without implicating Linda and telling his unknown enemy that he had recovered what might be a clue to the real story behind his father's death. There seemed to be no hope for him whatever.

Nevertheless, he worked systematically and hard at trying to loose his hands. He tried to twist loose until his wrists were raw and he even tried the expedient of sawing the tough rope on the edge of a log. This latter brought Dirk to the door to watch with that half sneer on his lips, and, after carefully inspecting the room for something sharper and failing to find it, to return to the kitchen without even warning Jim to desist. After which, seeing the futility of his efforts, Randall sat down again and gave himself over to gloomy thoughts.

In her bedroom in the far wing, Linda sat at the window and gazed out over the moondrenched rangeland. She held the tally book in her lap and there was a strange uneasiness in her heart. Her father had told her that nothing had been stolen, and Jim Randall had said that all he had come after was this book of his father's. Now he had been captured and would surely go to prison unless—

But he couldn't escape. Her father had told her of the precautions which had been taken to make the leanto escape-proof, and that Jeff Dirk himself intended to watch until morning. The thing that disturbed her was the knowledge that while Jim might be guilty under man's law, he wasn't under God's law. He had simply raised a window and had come in and got something that was rightfully his. She held the proof of it right here in her lap. But if this little book really contained evidence of his father's innocence it must not be shown prematurely. The only thing that she could do, and the thing that Jim had asked her to do, was to put it in a safe place and keep it for him. This she would do at the very first opportunity.

She went over to the bed and tucked it beneath the mattress, then returned to the window. She was not a bit sleepy, and Jim's problem, his unswerving loyalty to his father, intrigued and moved her. When would he come to her for the book? Not for months, maybe years, if they sent him to prison. And they would!

The minutes ticked by and became an hour and still she sat there. The moon was waning and soon the eastern sky would be filled with the glory of sunrise. The cook would be stirring and the men would eat and saddle their horses and take their prisoner out of the woodshed and ride away with him in their midst, bound like a criminal.

"No!" The whispered word was forced from between her lips. "No! He doesn't deserve that. He did it for the father he loved and respected just as I love and respect mine."

A sudden energy possessed her; she got up and dressed in blouse and riding skirt, keeping on her feet the soft slippers she wore. Stealing to the door she opened it quietly, stood there for several moments listening. There was no sound, and her heart beating wildly she tiptoed into the hall and from there to the livingroom. The window through which Jim had entered was still open; rather than risk making a noise unbarring the door she raised herself to the sill and thrust her feet through the opening. She heard the rasp of Dirk's chair in the kitchen and froze; then she heard him yawn and settle into silence again. She swung outside and stood on the gallery. Not a thing within range of her vision stirred, not a sound reached her.

Heart racing, she descended to the ground and skirted the gallery. She rounded the front of the house, passed the dark dining room, stood watching the light in the kitchen window for a second or two, then circled so as to approach the leanto from the rear.

She stole to the heavy four-by-four timber which braced the door, grasped it, tried to raise it. She might just as well have tried to raise the earth itself. With a smothered exclamation of despair she stepped back a pace and studied it. The stake at its foot was the key, she decided. She bent over and grasped it and tugged, gently at first, then with all her strength. It gave a grudging fraction of an inch. This much gained, she resumed her efforts, moving it in infinitesimal circles, feeling it gradually work loose under her hands. She gripped it tightly and tried to draw it out of the ground, failed, and worked at it some more.

And then she saw Dirk pass the lighted kitchen window and knew he was walking towards the door into the woodshed. Like a startled fawn she leaped back into the shadow, then stopped. She couldn't fail Jim now! She heard Jeff remove the bar, heard his gruff, "What are you trying to do, Randall?" and knew he had gone into the leanto.

She ran back to the stake, seized it and put her weight against it, once more wedging the timber securely against the spike in the door. She felt the shudder as Dirk tried it, pressed as hard as she could to keep the stake from giving. She heard him grunt and return to the kitchen, heard the bar drop into place across the door, saw him pass again by the lighted window.

She straightened, aware of a sudden weakness. It took all her will power to recover her composure. Again she worked at the stake; it resisted her efforts to draw it from the ground. Then she discovered the way to do it. Pulling it as far away from the end of the timber as she could, she seized the four-by-four at its base and dragged it sideways until the end was free of the stake.

And now came the most difficult part of her task. She couldn't simply push the timber away from the door and let it fall because of the noise it would make. She put her young shoulders under its middle and raised until it was off the ground. The end against the door grated along the wood and unbalanced her, and she sagged beneath its weight. Dimly she heard sounds inside the house, the scrape of Dirk's chair, the pound of his boots on the floor as he ran to the door, the rasp of the bar as he removed it.

She staggered sideways and let the heavy timber fall; then, almost sobbing in her anxiety, she ran blindly towards the front of the house and the opened window. She had done her best; Jim's fate was in the hands of Providence.

He needed the help of that omnipotent power. The first faint scratchings at the door had aroused him from his apathy like a dash of cold water; he came to his feet and only sank back as he heard Dirk approach. When Jeff entered the room he sat hunched on the stack of wood and when Dirk tried the door he was afraid to look up.

Jeff returned to the kitchen and the scraping was resumed; and suddenly it became so loud and continuous that Jim knew his guard must have heard it. He got up and leaped towards the doorway even as Dirk was wrenching the bar from its sockets. Then came the crash of the fallen timber and at the same time light flooded the leanto as Dirk pulled open the kitchen door.

Jim struck the outer door with all his weight and burst it open. He sprang through the entrance, heard the crash of Dirk's gun behind him, wheeled sharply to his right and was around the rear corner of the shed before Dirk could get outside.

He ran as he had never run before, heading for the shadows at the foot of the towering hills, but with his hands tied behind him he felt as though he were moving at a snail's pace. He didn't look back, but he could hear Dirk shouting for his men.

Jim ran on, working again at his bonds until he realized that by doing so he was rapidly losing ground. He headed now for the place where he had left his horse, thankful that he had tied the animal securely. Behind him he left confusion. He came upon the horse at last, turned his back and with numb fingers worked loose the knot in the reins. He could see horsemen fanning out on the moonlit range, heading unerringly towards him. He couldn't mount here; holding the reins tightly he started running again, dragging the horse behind him. His eyes searched swiftly for a rock; a log, something on which to stand.

A gun roared and he heard the whine of lead. The horse heard it also and increased its pace. Panting, stumbling over brush, Jim reached the line of trees. Here at least pursuit would be slowed. They were firing steadily now, their lead clipping branches and thudding into trees. The faintness of the rapidly dying moonlight was the only thing that saved Jim.

Jim stumbled often as he worked his way back into the brush, for here it was quite dark and he could not see where he was going. He brought up with a suddenness that bruised his legs, and the next instant gave an exclamation of relief. It was the trunk of a fallen tree into which he had crashed.

He climbed upon it, twisting his body, wasted precious seconds working the puzzled horse into position. The brush crashed to the hoofs of pursuers, but they too were working in the dark. Then the animal was where he wanted him and Jim leaped. He hit the saddle squarely, struck the horse's flanks sharply with his heels. The animal bounded away through the trees.

Linda was up when the crew returned from their search, led by a sullen Jeff Dirk. A quick glance told her that Jim Randall was not in their midst, and at breakfast Dirk savagely admitted that he had gotten away. "But we'll round him up," he declared. "As soon as the boys eat we're going after him again. He can't get far."

Linda felt a glow within her. Jim Randall had escaped and they would not catch him. She finished her breakfast and as soon as Dirk had gone with his crew to resume the search she saddled up and rode to Briscoe. Her father, dividing his time between the Star and the bank, would not go to town until the afternoon. When she entered the bank, Jason Rudd came from behind the grille to meet her. She said, "I have a package I'd like Mr. Dunham to take care of for me."

"Of course, Linda. He'll be glad to do it, I'm sure. Go right into his office."

Linda thanked him and entered the office bearing the letter-
ing VICE-PRESIDENT on its door. Dunham got up to greet her.

"Mr. Dunham, I've a package I wish you'd put in a safe place
for me. And please don't say anything to father about it. It—well,
it's a little secret that I don't want him to know about. Do you
think you can manage it for me?"

Dunham's face was politely grave. "Certainly, Miss Lane. I'll
be glad to. I'll put it in the vault."

"Don't mark it with my name, please; just put it where you
can get it quickly when I want it."

He nodded, took the flat parcel, turned it over in his hands.
"A book of some kind? Judging from the size I'd say a tally book."

"That's what it is. You'll take care of it for me? Thank you."
She gave him a smile and went out.

When she had gone, Dunham turned the package over in
his hands, examining the wrapping. Then he took it over to his
desk.

The Star Crew had breakfast, then rode out on the search
again with Jeff Dirk leading them. A short time before, Dirk's
troubles seemed at an end, with Randall a prisoner and the certain knowledge that he would be sent to prison; now his escape
had robbed Jeff of his triumph and would undoubtedly bring
the condemnation of the one who was so anxious to be rid of
Randall.

Around noontime the men began to grumble. They couldn't
see the sense of such an intensive and persistent search for a mere
housebreaker, and they wanted their dinner.

Dirk told them curtly, "You'll skip dinner today. I'm going
to round up Randall if I have to take these hills apart a stone
at a time. I've got to go to Briscoe and while I'm there I'll comb
the town for him. Lafe, you're in charge. Work towards that old
shanty of Bill Scott's and don't miss a thing. I'll meet you this
evening with a packload of grub. If you catch sight of Randall,
let him have it."

"Ain't that pilin' it on a bit heavy?" one of them wanted to know. "The feller didn't get away with anything."

"He didn't break into the house to pass away the time."

"Didn't he?" It was a man named Schwingel who said it, and he said it with a knowing grin. "When I clumb through the window he was right near the gal's bedroom. Seems like I heard 'em whisperin' together before he hightailed."

Dirk's eyes flamed. "That'll be enough of that kind of talk! You know damned well you're lying."

The man knew no such thing, but he was awed by Dirk's sudden fury. He made a reluctant admission, "Well, I mighta been mistook."

"You were. He came to the house to steal something and he had Bill Scott outside to keep watch. It was Scott who turned him loose."

"You sure of that, Jeff?"

Dirk made an impatient gesture. "It couldn't have been anybody else. Who busted up Panhandle's play? Scott, playing drunk down there on the store steps but watching Randall's back the whole time. I aim to check up on him too, and if my hunch is good I know one prospector who's going to run into trouble in the hills and never show up again."

He reined his horse around and set out for Briscoe, and the crew went on with the search. On the trail to town Jeff met Linda on her way back to the Star and stopped her to talk, but she showed no desire to linger and rode on after the briefest of exchanges. Dirk frowned heavily when she left him, Schwingel's statement recurring to him. Was she really working with Randall? Was it she who had set him free? He considered it for a moment and finally decided that she was incapable of that.

The bank closed at four and by riding hard he made it with minutes to spare. He went directly into Dunham's office, leaving the door open. Both Brent Wood, who had been reinstated as teller, and Jason Rudd could hear the conversation.

Jeff said, "Hello, Lew. Guess you heard about Randall breaking into the Star house last night."

Dunham looked his astonishment. "No, I hadn't. Linda was here but she didn't say a word about it."

"She didn't? Well, we caught him redhanded and locked him in the leanto for the night. Fastened the outside door with a heavy timber and I sat in the kitchen to make sure he wouldn't get away. Somebody moved the timber and let him out, and right now he's loose in the hills. My crew is tracking him down and I'm pretty sure they'll get him."

"Your crew couldn't catch Jim Randall if he was out on the open range under a noon sun," said Dunham flatly. "And if they do happen to run into him he'd probably shoot half of them and send the other half flying. Did he get anything?"

"He didn't have time."

"Search him?"

"Yes. I reckon you can move those yearlings back on his place; he'll be afraid to come back with a long jail term staring him in the face."

"I think I'll wait a spell," said Dunham drily. "You assured me once before that he wouldn't be back. Got any idea who let him out?"

"My hunch says it was Bill Scott."

"Scott? What time was it when he got away?"

"Around four this morning."

"Then you better find a new hunch. I stayed at the hotel last night and was up at six. Scott was waiting for the bar to open. That burrow of his couldn't have made it from the Star to town in two hours if it had wings instead of feet."

"You sure of that?"

"Positive. He was sitting on the hotel steps at six this morning."

Dirk got up from his chair, his face tight. "Well, that's one of the reasons I came in—to check up on him." He nodded and walked out of the bank.

The frown had returned, and within him burned a mounting anger. Scott hadn't freed Jim Randall, so perhaps Schwingel hadn't lied after all. If he had heard Jim talking with Linda in the hallway, it could have been the girl who had released Randall. Why? The only reason Dirk could find in his jealous mind was that the girl was in love with Randall. The thought was not a cheering one...

Up in the hills, Bill Scott slid from his burro's back, walked quickly to the cabin, threw open the door and glanced around. Then he went to the corner and called in the general direction of the grove of trees behind the shack, "All right, you danged loon! Come on out."

Jim rode into the open and stepped to the ground. Scotty said, "Ain't you got no sense a-tall. comin' here? Don't you know the whole Star crew is out gunnin' for you and will hit for here directly? By gob, if they ketch up with you they'll make a Swiss cheese outa you."

"I can do some cheese making myself. I've a good horse, a rifle and your extra sixgun."

"And they got eight good horses, eight rifles and eight sixguns. You got to get outa here quick. Keep your eye peeled while I round up some grub."

He darted into the cabin to return presently with blankets and a gunny sack filled with supplies.

"Here; hang these on your saddle and let's light out. I know a place where you'll be safe. What in the thunderin' Gehenna made you bust into the Star house anyway?"

"Where'd you hear about it?"

"In town. Everybody's talkin' about it."

Jim answered as he fastened the supplies in place. "I had a hunch, Scotty; a mighty good hunch." He went on to tell of the finding of the tally book. "I'm betting that dad wrote something in there that'll give us a clue."

"Where is it?"

"I gave it to Linda Lane to keep for me."

"Linda! Now I know you're loco! Why, her old man manages the Star; he's in this up to his neck."

"I don't think so. Anyhow, I had no choice. It looked like I couldn't possibly get away and I didn't want them to get hold of that tally book. And say! I found the address of the lawyer that Lane writes to."

"You did? Feller, right now that's more important than the tally book. You give me that address and I'll sic our detective feller on him. Hurry up and get on your hoss; we're goin' to make some fancy tracks out of here."

They mounted and Scotty took the lead, angling higher into the hills and carrying on a conversation over his shoulder. "Our hunch about Dunham sure looks better and better. Jeff Dirk went straight to him and told him the story. I seen him go into the bank and snuck around in the back. Dunham had his winder open and I heard it all." He chuckled. "He thinks it was me turned you loose."

"Nothing strange about that."

"No—'ceptin' it ain't true."

"You mean it wasn't you? Who was it then?"

"Who'd you give the tally book to?"

"Linda?" He thought a moment, his pulse quickening. He shook his head. "Nothing doing, Scotty. She couldn't handle that heavy timber or pull the stake that held it against the door. And she wouldn't even dare try. Or would she?"

"Well, I didn't, and it's a cinch Alonzo didn't, and we know Jeff didn't, and you ain't got any friends on the crew that I know of. Sure she done it."

For a while Jim rode in silence, but his blood was pounding and his eyes were shining.

At the end of two hours Scotty pulled up his burro in the dry bed of a brush-choked gully. "We'll have to handle this right careful, Jim. Back of them bushes is a drift I once drove into the arroyo bank; if we can find a way of gettin' you and the hoss into it without disturbin' the surroundin' scenery too much, a whole flock of Satan's angels couldn't find you."

They made their way into the drift without too much effort, and Jim found himself in a passage way so low that he had to dismount in order to clear the dirt roof.

"Here you are," said Scotty, and lighted a candle he took from a niche in the wall. "And here you're goin' to stay while I get in touch with our detective feller and do another chore I have in mind. You got grub enough to last you a week and there's a spring a hundred yards down the gully. They's some oats in that sack, but you'll hafta picket the hoss at night down hear the spring. If you git lonesome you can exchange sweet nothin's with the critter. I want you to stay right here until I come for you."

"How long is that going to be?"

"If I ain't back in a week you're on your own."

"A week! Scotty, I'll die if I have to hole up here for a week."

"You'll sure enough die if you don't. Jeff Dirk ain't foolin' none; he's out to get you and I'm bettin' his men have orders to shoot you on sight. Naw, sir; you stay put until I git back."

"A week!" groaned Jim. "Scotty, you get that tally book from Linda and come humping right back here with it."

"I'll git the tally book, all right, but I ain't gonna be in no big hurry about it. Lew Dunham told Dirk I couldn't have turned you loose, he havin' seen me in Briscoe at the time. Well, you can bet Jeff asked hisself right off what other friend of yours was handy to do it, and there ain't but one answer to that. He'll be hopin' to find you by keepin' tabs on her, and I'll have to git in touch with her when he ain't around. No, sir; you lay low and leave the rest to me."

Meanwhile, Jeff Dirk had returned to the Star around dusk and he had to hustle to get together supplies, pack them and transport them to his men before they mutinied and returned to the ranch. He found them camped in a draw near a spring, dispirited and hungry. Two of them set out at once to prepare their long delayed supper, and while they were about it the man called Lafe made his report.

"No luck so far, Jeff. We snuck up on that old shack of Scott's but it was empty. Plenty of tracks, some recent. If Randall was there, he's gone."

"Keep at it," said Dirk tersely. "Have the men take turns scouting around tonight. We'll run down that fox yet."

He rode back to the ranch determined to get another matter off his chest. Linda and her father were sitting on the gallery and he joined them. After a while Alonzo Lane bade them goodnight and went inside the house.

"You're not in very good humor," Linda told him. "It must be that your search for Jim isn't going so well."

"We'll find him," promised Jeff grimly. "Find him or chase him so far he'll never come back."

Linda, remembering another occasion, said softly, "Want to bet?"

He turned to her angrily. "Linda, why did you let him out of that shed?"

He had expected to surprise her, but she had expected that this question would be asked sooner or later. She said quietly, "Because I knew you intended to send him to prison for no reason at all except that you hate him and want to hurt him."

Her frankness jarred him. "For no reason! Good heavens, girl! He broke into your house in the dead of night and you sit there and say that!"

"He didn't steal anything, did he?"

"Only because he didn't have time."

"He had all the time he needed. I happen to know that he didn't break in to steal."

"You know, do you?" grated Dirk, and in his anger proceeded to make the grand mistake of his lifetime. "Perhaps you're going to tell me that he paid the visit at your suggestion? I seem to remember your asking him to call."

He knew at once that he had gone entirely too far, but was too angry and stubborn to retract his words immediately. Linda said nothing, and in the darkness he could not see her; but he felt her eyes steadily upon him and the contempt in them burned through the gloom. Before he could anticipate the action she had got to her feet and had gone into the house.

He started after her with a beseeching, "Linda! Don't go! I'm sorry; I didn't mean a word of it." But he was too late; the door had closed and he heard the bar fall into place. For a few seconds he stood there, fists clenched at his sides, face burning with humiliation; then with a fervent curse he turned and strode off the gallery.

Thereafter he took personal charge of the man hunt until even Alonzo Lane rebuked him for neglecting the ranch work. By that time nearly a week had passed and his men had become sick and tired of the endless task. He told himself that this time Jim Randall had surely left the country and called off the search leaving quite a few of the stones he had promised to turn remaining in place.

And at the end of that week Jim Randall stood at the mouth of the drift, one hand holding the rein of his saddled horse. Scotty had said that at the end of a week he was on his own, and that week had dragged by like a month and now he was free to take what steps he thought necessary to recover the precious tally book.

He stood there for some minutes listening and peering about through the screening underbrush. Just the day before Dirk's men had come near and he supposed they were still searching for him. He was about to move into the open when he heard a sound farther up the gully and noiselessly backed his horse into the drift and drew his rifle from the boot.

The sounds drew nearer and he knew they were made by the hoofs of horses. Backing farther into the drift, he levered a cartridge into the Winchester and crouched with it half levelled. Straight to the entrance came the horsemen, twisting through the tortuous passage which led to his hideout. Then came Scotty's voice. "All right, Jim! Come on out."

Randall released a sigh of relief and went to the entrance. Scotty had dismounted, and sitting their horses were four grinning men.

"Reckon you know these rannies," said the old man. "They worked for your dad and worked for him a good many years. I went me on a still hunt and rounded 'em up. This yere drammer's drawin' along towards the last act and I figgered we'd need 'em before the curtain come down."

CHAPTER SEVEN

RANDALL STRODE forward with a glad exclamation, greeting them in turn as they dropped to the ground. There were Tiny Blossom, six-feet-two high and two-feet-six wide; Idaho Webb, longfaced and serious-eyed, with the grace of a puma and the strength of a lion; Sam Staley, expert with rifle, rope and six-gun; and Juan the Mexican, dark and debonair, with a hand equally facile at plucking a guitar or pulling a trigger. They were the cream of the old Star crew.

"You old hellions!" cried Jim. "Where did Scotty find you?"

"Took me a week," said Scotty. "They'd drifted some."

"Me, I'm theenk you're not come back," grinned Juan.

"We all hung around for three months," said Tiny, "then we had to move on or starve. Dunham had a full crew and Jeff Dirk fetched his own men. Gosh, Jim, I'm sure glad to see you."

Idaho Webb drawled, "Scotty tells me you ain't swallerin' all that pap about John shootin' hisself. He says you aim to find the gent that framed him and nail his hide to the fence. I'd admire to drive some nails myself."

"When Scotty showed me the layout you're buckin'," put in Sam Staley, "I figgered immediate that four aces might fill your hand for you. You got no chance in a game just holdin' one card. What do we do first?"

"We eat," said Tiny. "My stomach thinks my throat's been cut. Where's the mess shack, Jim?"

Randall's eyes were bright and there was a smile on his lips. He could face any opposition with these men to back him and not ask odds. "We eat on my place, the old Star line camp. Let's go!"

"Now looky yere," protested Scotty. "Dirk's crew is still on the prod and if they ketch sight of you they ain't gonna throw spitballs."

Jim was already on his horse. "Whatever they throw they're going to get it tossed right back at them. They've mauled me and broken my bones and danged near buried me alive when I was sitting in the game with only one card. Now that I've filled my hand I aim to push in the blue chips. What did you do about the Philadelphia lawyer, Scotty?"

"I sicked our detective feller on him. He'll let us know soon's he finds out somethin'."

"And the tally book?"

"Ain't had no time to git it yet. I figgered I'd better round up the boys first."

"We've got to have it, Scotty. If there isn't something mighty interesting in it I'll eat it without salt. Come on, boys; let's go."

They reached the homestead without encountering any of Dirk's men and found the place deserted. The supplies Jim had bought were still there and Scotty lost no time in preparing dinner. When they had eaten, Jim gave the old fellow his instructions. "I want you to go to Briscoe and wait there until Miss Linda comes in. Give her this note and she'll get the tally book for you."

Scotty set out on his burro and had hardly passed out of sight when Juan, who had elected to do a little scouting, came sweeping over the ridge. Jim and the other three came outside to hear the news he had for them.

"I'm theenk we 'ave the fon," grinned Juan. "The Senor Dun'am ees come weeth two *hombres* and some *vacas*."

"Driving them over again, eh?" said Jim grimly. "He'll walk them plumb off their hoofs between here and the Box D before he gets it through his head that this is no free pasture."

"We shoot, make 'em ron, no?" said Juan eagerly.

"No, Juan, we don't shoot until they start shooting. Take your horse around back and then go into the cabin. You fellows go with him. I'll stay here. I want you to hear what he has to say."

They did as he ordered and had scarcely got out of sight when the first yearlings came over the ridge. Dunham himself was riding point, and Jim saw him halt abruptly at sight of a man seated in front of the cabin. Lew called to one of his men, who rode up and proceeded to hold the cattle while Dunham loped his horse up to the cabin.

"Howdy, Lew," greeted Jim quietly.

Dunham nodded. "I should have known it; I told Dirk—Look here, Jim, aren't you taking pretty big chances in coming back? The Star is gunning for you and this time the law's on their side. You *did* break into the Star ranchhouse, didn't you?"

"Yes, but all I took was something my father had left there."

"Hm-m-m. It wasn't by any chance a tally book, was it?"

"It might be."

"Read it yet?"

"No. It's in a safe place; I can get it when I need it. And I expect to find something mighty interesting in it, Lew."

Dunham smiled faintly. "If you're counting on it to prove your father was innocent I think you'll be disappointed." He studied Jim thoughtfully for a moment. "You certainly are a stubborn cuss, aren't you?" he asked; then, when Jim did not answer, he wheeled his horse and rejoined his men on the crest of the ridge, and presently the herd vanished from sight on its way to home range. Jim's four companions came out to join him.

"He's a mighty good guesser, ain't he?" said Idaho.

"Too danged good," answered Sam. "How'd he know it was a tally book you found?"

"That's easy," explained Tiny. "Lew's vice-president of the bank and Lane's president. The girl told her father and he told Lew."

Jim frowned. He had hoped that Linda would keep his secret, but it looked very much as though Tiny's explanation was correct. It became doubly important now that he secure the tally book before Dunham managed to get it from Linda—if he hadn't already got it.

He was debating what to do about this new development when he heard the roll of hoofs beyond the spur of hill which cut off his view of the Star, and immediately ordered the others inside the cabin again. Four horsemen swept into view and Jim recognized them as Jeff Dirk and Panhandle's three pals. At sight of him they let out a shout of triumph and one of them let fly with his six-gun. The bullet fell short, and Jim saw Dirk turn to the man who had fired it with an evident order to hold his fire. The four of them advanced slowly, drawing their rifles from their saddle boots.

Tiny's voice came from the cabin behind Jim in a whispered, "Want us to discourage 'em, Jim?"

Jim answered without turning his head. "No. Just keep them covered. Let's hear what they have to say."

The four came on slowly, warily, spreading out a bit as they did so. Jim sat on the bench and calmly smoked on, confident that his men would take care of any precipitate development. A dozen yards away from Jim, Dirk halted his horse and his companions drew up in a little half-circle facing Randall. Dirk said, "So you decided to come back and face the music. I don't know why, but it's jake with me. Stand up, Randall, and put your hands in the air." He swept his rifle around to cover Jim.

Randall was enjoying himself. For some reason he found a grim pleasure in belittling this arrogant man. He answered calmly. "I came back, but I don't intend to give myself up."

"If you don't," said Jeff tersely, "I'll have every reason in the world for shooting you like a sitting duck."

"I wouldn't try it," said Jim calmly. "If you even look like it you're going out in a blaze of glory." He raised his voice. "Tiny! Sam! Idaho! Juan!"

Dirk's eyes went swiftly to the cabin behind Jim. Two men had come into sight in the doorway, and two more were leaning from the window. All four had rifles, and each rifle was levelled at a horseman.

Jim said, "If you wanted to see me about anything, Dirk, speak up. If you just called out of curiosity, start laying down tracks."

Dirk's face darkened and his eyes smouldered; but he lowered the rifle slowly until its muzzle was pointing at the ground. He said, "So you called in the army, huh? All right, Randall; this is your trick, but it's not the last in the game. Don't forget that." He turned to his men, jerked his head towards the range and reined his horse about. The other three backed away slowly, then wheeled and raced after him, heading for the protection of the projecting spur of hill.

"Goin' for reinforcements, I hope," said Idaho Webb.

"Let him fetch 'em," said Tiny. "We got a good stout log cabin here and plenty of grub and water. Let 'em come!"

They got ready for attack, fetching their horses to the leanto, seeing to their food and water and ammunition; then, with Juan riding about to give them warning, the other four sat down to a game of poker.

Supper time came without the expected attack and Jim prepared a meal for them. He was aching for action but there was nothing they could do until the tally book had been read. When darkness fell they did not light the lamp, but Sam Staley saddled up and went out to help Juan stand guard, and Jim and Idaho and Tiny sat on the bench and talked.

At last they heard the plod of hoofs and Juan rode up with Scotty. The old man slid from his burro and handed Jim a wrapped parcel. "Here she is," he said. "Linda was buyin' some stuff at the store and I slipped her your note. She went out and I seen her go into the bank. When she come out she had this. Reckon Alonzo was keepin' it for her."

Jim led the way into the cabin and lighted the lamp. Removing the paper he disclosed the tally book, and one quick look at the first page showed his father's familiar writing. He noticed that the book was kept in diary form, with each entry carefully dated. The record had been started five years before.

He skipped over the first three-quarters of it, reaching at last the date when the bank was first opened. The others crowded about him, reading over his shoulder.

"Look here," Jim said, and quoted an entry. " 'Scotty came in to borrow a hundred, claiming he'd located a likely prospect. Of course I let him have it. He wanted to give me his note but I wouldn't take it. Scotty's word is better than a whole bale of legal paper. I wish him luck.' "

"By gob!" cried Scotty.

Jim was thumbing through the pages. "Yes, here it is. 'Scotty came in today and paid me the hundred he'd borrowed. Wanted to give me half of what he found, claiming I had grubstaked him. I told the old coot that was a bank loan and not a grubstake, and charged him six percent interest to shut him up.' "

There were other entries recording small loans. Mention was made of some repayments, but there were many running like, "Jake Billings offered me five dollars on his loan. His wife had been sick and he was up against it. I told him to pay me when he could better afford it." Or, "Ed Cornish's house burned down last night. The poor fellow lost everything. I lent him five hundred and told him not to worry about paying it back in a hurry. Took his note but mislaid it somewhere."

"Anybody who'd say that man's a thief is a damned liar!" blazed Tiny.

"Wait!" cried Jim suddenly. "Listen to this! 'Took a little flyer on some stock a short time ago and received word today that the company had gone bust. Never did believe in speculation but was talked into this. Not much loss. Got a few other irons in the fire but after this won't count on any handsome profits.' "

"Keep a-readin'," urged Scotty, "and mebbe we'll git a line on them big investments he's supposed to have made."

But no further entry concerning speculation was found except for one brief item. "Got a wire from Chicago asking for more margin. I wired back to sell out and close the account. No more get-rich-quick schemes for me."

"There!" cried Scotty. "There wasn't no more investments! By gob, this thing is gittin' more smelly by the minute!"

"Yes, we're certainly getting somewhere," Jim told them, and pointed to the last entry. " 'Lew came in all serious and jacked me up about lending money without security. Said Jason couldn't keep his books straight and didn't know where the bank stood. He was so all-fired upset that I told him to have Jason make an audit and I'd give him a note for any shortage. By the way he acted a person would have thought—' " Jim broke off. He had reached the bottom of the page and the next one was blank. He thumbed the pages, but they were blank clear to the end of the book.

"That's funny," he said, and examined the crease in the middle of the book. "Fellows, there's a page missing. Cut out."

"Why'd he cut it out?" asked Tiny.

"Dang it, he didn't!" answered Scotty. "If he hadn't wanted what he'd written seen, he wouldn't have writ it in the first place. Somebody's cut out that there page *because it gives the clue we've been huntin' for!*"

"You say Linda got it from the bank," said Jim sharply. "I reckon we know now how Lew Dunham learned it was a tally book."

"Why, the low-down louse!"

Jim got to his feet. "I'm tired of pussyfooting. First thing in the morning, we're riding over to the bank and have a little chat with Mr. Lewis Dunham."

Immediately after breakfast they started for town, matching the pace of Scotty's burro, and sighted Briscoe around ten.

Scotty lagged behind, not wishing to impair his usefulness by appearing too closely associated with Randall, and Jim and his four punchers rode boldly down the main street and dismounted outside the bank. Jeff Dirk watched them from inside the store, and when he saw Jim enter he left in search of Marshal Mosley.

Brent Wood nodded a surprised greeting and said, "Hello, Jim; what can we do for you?"

"Is Mr. Lane in?"

"No, he isn't. He usually stays out at the ranch in the morning and comes to the bank in the afternoon. Anything I can do?"

"About a week ago Miss Lane left a package with him to keep for her; do you know anything about it?"

"I know she left a parcel, but not with Mr. Lane. She gave it to Lew and he put it in the vault. She got it yesterday."

"You say she gave it to Lew?"

"That's right, Jim."

Randall turned to his men, who had followed him into the bank. "Wait here, boys," he said, and pushed open the door labeled VICE-PRESIDENT and walked in, closing the door behind him. Dunham was seated with his back to the desk staring through the window, but as Jim entered he swung around and for once his face lost its professional calm in an expression of surprise.

"You here? Randall, I admire nerve in a man but you're carrying it too far. You're just asking for trouble by coming to Briscoe."

"That's right, Lew; and I'm ready for it."

Dunham shrugged. "What do you want?"

"An explanation from you about that tally book."

"You've read it?"

"Yes. I know now why you were so sure I'd be disappointed. The last page is missing, cut out of the book."

Dunham glared at him. "And you're accusing me—?"

"You just bet I am! Otherwise, how'd you know that I'd be disappointed? How'd you know it was a tally book to begin with?"

"I knew it was a tally book," answered Dunham coldly, "because of its shape and size and also because your father had mentioned using one as a sort of diary. Linda Lane asked me to keep it for her and I put it in the vault and left it there until yesterday, when she called for it."

Jim came over to the desk and leaned his hands on its top. "Lew, it's my hunch that that missing page held the clue to my father's murder."

"I told you before and I tell you again that he wasn't murdered. He committed suicide. All the evidence points to it and you're just too stubborn to admit it."

"All the evidence doesn't point to it. Lew, I found a corner of my mother's picture in the fireplace ashes. That's one thing Dad never would have burned. The one who did burn it killed my father."

"Fine evidence!" sneered Dunham. "See how far it'll get you with the sheriff and prosecuting attorney!"

The sneer infuriated Jim and he was goaded to say more than he had intended to. "I'll promise you that it'll get me a damned sight farther than you think when I hook it up with some other facts I've discovered! The Acme Cattle Company, for instance. It's supposed to be a big outfit with headquarters in Philadelphia, isn't it? That being the case, it's mighty queer that the Chief of Police in that city can't locate any such firm or find anybody who ever heard of it!"

"What's that?" It was plain that Dunham had been jarred.

"You heard me, Lew. Yes, I've dug up quite a few facts, but here's something that I haven't found out yet: Where were you on the night my father was killed?"

"Where was I?" Dunham's face purpled and he half rose from his chair; then, by an evident effort of his will, he gained control of himself and slowly sank back again. "So you're trying to pin this so-called murder on me eh? Well, you can't do it. It happens that I rode up to the Argosy Mine to see about a shipment of bullion and spent the night with the superintendent, George Campbell. Try getting around that, Randall."

"It probably won't be easy. The skunk that did it got himself all surrounded with alibis, but I'm going to smoke him out of his hole as sure as you're a foot high." He turned on his heel and strode from the office. The four punchers as well as Brent Wood and Jason Rudd were staring at him and he realized that their raised voices must have been heard.

"Come on, boys," he said shortly, and led the way from the bank. As he stepped through the doorway he felt the nudge of a Colt against his ribs and turned his head to see Marshal Jeb Mosley.

Jeb said, "You're under arrest, Randall."

"What for?"

"For bustin' into the Star ranch. Better come along without any trouble."

"You got a warrant?"

"Don't need none."

"Has Mr. Lane charged me with breaking and entering?"

"Don't make any difference whether he has or not. You done it."

"It makes a lot of difference. You're a town marshal; what happened out at the Star is out of your jurisdiction. And if I haven't been charged with any crime, you or nobody else can arrest me."

Tiny came out of the bank and after him the other three. "That's right," Tiny told Mosley. "Better pull that smokepole out of Jim's ribs; you're ticklin' him."

Mosley was taken aback. Jeff Dirk hadn't told him there were five of them; he had merely said, "Randall's in the bank; better nab him on his way out." The marshal now knew why Jeff hadn't accompanied him and resented being put in a ridiculous position. He lowered his gun. "If you're goin' to make a point of law of it, all right; but I'm warnin' you Randall, and this goes for your men, too; don't start anything in Briscoe. You'll sure enough be in my territory if you do."

He nodded for emphasis and strode off the steps, shoving his gun back into its holster.

Jim motioned to his men and got on his horse. "Reckon you heard most of the argument between Dunham and me. We're riding to the Argosy to see the superintendent and check on his alibi."

As they rode out of town, Jeff Dirk came from the store, went into the bank and spoke to Lew Dunham through the open doorway. "What was Randall doing in here?"

Dunham answered coldly. "He was here on business. You're not much of a prophet, Jeff; you said he wouldn't come back."

Dirk swore harshly. "He wouldn't have if he hadn't picked up those four roughs somewhere. I've a mind to take our outfit over and force a showdown now that I got the law on our side."

"Better ride over to Hartsville and get the sheriff to deputize you," advised Dunham. "Then when he shoots up your crew you can call in the army."

"That might not be a bad idea," snapped Dirk. "He's made it a personal issue and this town's getting too small to hold us both." He turned away, then halted as Linda came into the bank. Her eyes were flashing and her chin was in the air and Jeff knew by these signs that trouble was brewing. She swept past him without even a nod of greeting and walked to the doorway of Dunham's office. "Mr. Dunham," she said tightly, "I'd like to speak to you privately."

"Of course. Come in and close the door."

She went in and for a few minutes there was silence except for the low murmur of their voices; then Dunham's door opened and he spoke. "Rudd, you and Wood come in here a moment, will you?"

The two went into the office and once more the door was closed. Dirk, busy making a cigarette, looked quickly around, saw that he was alone in the banking room, and moved quietly to the door, listening.

Inside the room, Dunham spoke gravely to Brent Wood and Jason Rudd. "A week ago Miss Lane gave me a parcel to keep for her. I put it into the vault. Have either of you tampered with it?"

Rudd looked wonderingly at Brent Wood.

"Certainly not," said Wood, his cheeks flushing.

Dunham's gaze went to Rudd, who shook his head somberly. "I saw the parcel, of course, but I knew you'd put it there and I didn't even touch it."

"Somebody did," Linda told them shortly. "It was a book, what you call a tally book, and the last page is missing."

"You're sure, Miss Lane," said Rudd deferentially, "that the page wasn't gone when you gave it to Mr. Dunham?"

"I'm quite sure. You see, I did something which perhaps was wrong. The book was in the form of a diary written by Mr. John Randall. It was given to me by Jim Randall to keep for him. He hadn't had time to read it, but was certain that it contained some clue to his father's death. He believes, you know, that his father was murdered." Her gaze rested on each of them in turn. "I'm beginning to believe it too, and, knowing that if that was so the killer would make every effort to get that book, I read the entries before I wrapped it and gave it to Mr. Dunham."

"And you found—?" prompted Dunham.

"I found one entry on the last page—the missing page—which needs explaining. I haven't told a soul what it was, not even my father; but I intend to tell Jim Randall just as soon as I can find him. Bill Scott told me of the missing page just a minute ago, and it was my intention to ride straight out to Jim's homestead, but Scotty said that they hadn't passed him on their way home and the liveryman said he'd seen them riding towards the south hills, so I'll have to wait until they return. I don't know who cut out that page and I haven't the slightest idea who killed John Randall; but I do know from that missing page that John Randall was not a thief and my belief that he was murdered was strengthened. Whoever destroyed that page hasn't gained a thing, for I'm going to pass its contents along to Jim Randall just as soon as I can get in touch with him. And that, I think, is all I have to say."

Jeff Dirk just managed to get out of the bank before she came out of the office...

George Campbell, superintendent of the Argosy, was a short, stocky man with heavy brows and a perpetual scowl, and the welcome he extended to Jim and his men was not a hearty one.

"Sure I remember the night John Randall kicked off," he said in answer to Jim's question. "I ought to; we carried an account with his bank and lost several thousands. What about it?"

"Did you see Lew Dunham that night?"

"See him? I slept with him. He came up to talk about a gold shipment and stayed over with me."

"What time did he get here?"

"Around supper time. He stayed with me until the next morning."

"Did anybody else see him?"

"I don't think so; not while he was here. I live alone and he came straight to my house. We had supper and then talked until late. When he started to leave I said he might as well bunk with me. He got up early the next morning, ate some breakfast and started back. Might have met somebody on the trail; I wouldn't know that."

It was all the information they could get out of George Campbell.

It was evening when they finally rode up to the cabin to find Scotty awaiting them with supper on the stove. The old fellow was keyed up with exictement. "Time you was show-in' up," he said. "Eat your supper and then git ready to ride over to the Star."

"The Star?"

"Yeah! Linda wants to see you powerful bad, Jim. Feller, our luck has changed. Yes, sir! I met her in town right after you'd started for the hills. Told her about the missin' page and was she mad! Bristled up like a she porky-pine and headed licketysplit for the bank. I cut around to Lew's winder in time to hear him call Brent Wood and Jason Rudd into the office... Here; set down and start feedin', and I'll talk while you're stuffin' yourselves... Lew tole 'em about the book she'd left with him to take care of and asked if either of 'em had monkeyed with it. They said no. 'Well,' says Linda, 'somebody did because the last page is missin'.' 'How do you know it wasn't missin' when you give it to Lew?' asks Jason. 'I know,' she says, 'because I read it.'

"Then she went on to tell 'em about your not believin' your father committed suicide and said she didn't believe it neither. She said you figgered that diary would bear it out. 'And what did you find when you read it?' asks Lew, cool as a cucumber. 'I found one entry that needs a lot of explainin',' she snapped at him. 'It told me that John Randall was no thief and makes me more sure than ever that he was killed, and I aim to tell Jim about it as soon as I can find him.' "

"Wow!" yelled Tiny, and got up so suddenly that he upset his coffee. "Let's go!"

The others came to their feet, suppers forgotten. In a bunch they made for the corral, Scotty hobbling behind them and yelling for them to wait for him. They caught up their horses, saddled them and headed for the Star. Jim's face was shining; more than ever he thanked his stars that he had given the book to Linda to keep.

He had half expected to meet her on the way over, but the trail was empty clear to the Star ranch house. They swept into the yard and pulled up at the gallery. The crew had finished supper some time before and four of them lounged in front of the bunkhouse. Jim ran up on the gallery and rapped on the door while his companions sat with ready rifles. Alonzo Lane answered Jim's knock.

"I'd like to speak to Miss Linda," Jim told Lane.

"Linda? She's not here. Haven't you seen her? She started for your place right after supper, about an hour ago."

CHAPTER EIGHT

J IM STARTED, the clammy hand of apprehension upon him. "You're sure she headed for my place?"

"Positive." Sudden anxiety appeared in Lane's face. "You just came from there? You didn't meet her?"

"No." Jim wheeled, leaped from the gallery and strode over to the bunkhouse. "Where's Dirk and the rest of the crew?"

"Left right after supper," answered one of the loungers. "Didn't say where they was goin'. To town, I reckon."

Jim returned to his companions, got into the saddle and led the way from the yard at a sharp lope.

"You reckon she went to Briscoe?" asked Tiny.

"No. She wanted to see me as soon as she could. She started for our place right after supper and Jeff Dirk and his three left about the same time."

"Looks to me," said Sam Staley grimly, "as though Dunham had Dirk get her out of the way so's she couldn't tell you what she found in that tally book."

Jim slowed to a walk. "Lane said she left an hour ago; that's just about the time we started from our place. That means she couldn't have covered more than half the distance when Jeff caught her. Start looking for a sign."

They searched diligently, but the swiftly gathering darkness hampered them and slowed their progress. Scotty arrived on his burro with the information that Linda had not put in appearance at the homestead, and he too was put to work. At last the darkness became so intense that there was danger of their missing the clues for which they sought and Jim called a halt.

"Build a fire," he ordered grimly. "Tiny, ride back to the cabin and get a couple of lanterns. Keep up the search. I'm going to Briscoe to find out if Jeff Dirk and his three pet polecats are there. If they're not, we'll know for sure what became of Linda and I'll gather a searching party that'll turn these hills inside out."

He started at once, riding swiftly. Town was two hours away and he did not spare his horse. Fear gripped him. Although he reasoned that no harm would come to Linda, just the thought of her in the hands of Dirk and his ruffians tortured him. The miles dragged and he drove his horse until realization reached him that the animal would never last if he kept up the furious pace. He slowed to a walk and held it for a full mile, then proceeded at a more reasonable gait. After a seeming eternity he sighted the lights of the town.

A mile ahead of him, just on the outskirts of the town, a horseman swung off the trail and angled for the alley which paralleled the main street. The rider's clothing was dark and he rode a dark bay horse; both man and beast were indistinguishable except when outlined against the slightly lighter sky.

There was a tumbledown bagin at the end of the street, and behind this an equally decrepit shed. At the latter the man dismounted and tied, then he removed his spurs, hung them on the saddle horn and started softly along the black alley, picking his way, dodging the occasional patches of light which filtered through back windows.

He came to an intersecting street, waited until he was sure there was nobody to see, then darted like a shadow to the far side. He brought up behind the brick structure which was the bank. For a short space he crouched against the wall, watching and listening; then he softly moved to the back steps, mounted them. A key grated and the door swung open. Silently he glided inside.

He was in the space behind the grilled partition. Along the wall to his left were filing cabinets and office equipment; in the middle of the room, he knew, was the bookkeeping desk. The partition to his right had a door opening into the office of the vice-president, which in turn connected with that of the president. Against the wall to the left stood the big vault. There was no time lock, but it was as burglar-proof as a safe could be made.

The man made his way to it, drew from a pocket a small bullseye lantern and, crouching close to the floor, risked lighting it. There was a momentary flare of light, then darkness again except for the thin gleam from the lantern. He stood up, let the ray slip along the front of the vault until it was centered on the combination dial. Quickly, methodically, he turned the dial until a tiny click told him the tumblers had fallen. Putting the lantern on the floor, he grasped the metal wheels and spun them. In the act of pulling open the heavy doors he stopped, his heart leaping into his throat. From somewhere behind him had come a sound.

He wheeled swiftly. He was no coward, but he knew that if the sound had been made by a certain person his doom was sealed. He wanted to say, "Who is that?" sharply, authoritatively, as one who is sure of his position and his right to be where he was; but the words wouldn't come. He had left the slide of the lantern open and was suddenly aware that his own shape must be dimly visible to anybody who stood in the deep shadows only an arm's length from him.

There was a soft footfall and he knew that he was trapped. Instinctively he braced himself. The blaze of a six-gun lighted the room and its heavy boom echoed like sullen thunder ...

When Jim Randall entered the town he pulled up at the first hitching rack he came to and slid from his wet horse. It was close to midnight and all places of business except the saloons were closed. There were six of these in Briscoe. He pushed through the doorway of the first, glanced quickly over the meager crowd, spoke tersely to a bartender. "Seen Jeff Dirk tonight?"

"Nope."

"Any of the Star crew?"

"Nope."

He went out, walked swiftly to the next one and tried again. He got the same answer; no Jeff Dirk, no Star men that night. At the third it was the same, also at the fourth. The other two saloons were located on the far side of the street, so he crossed the road and started back.

The fifth saloon brought him no better luck; the sixth and last was at the end of the street. Jim tramped steadily over the plank sidewalk, almost feeling his way in the blackness. He passed the stage station where George Finch's lack of welcome had surprised him on the occasion of his return from Montana. Across the street was the little shack which had until recently housed the real-estate office of Jason Rudd. Directly ahead of him, on the same side, was the bank.

His eyes were drawn to it by a sudden dull glow which lighted its back windows for a brief moment, and he stopped in surprise. Mechanically he glanced at the sky, saw the stars, and knew that the flash was not the reflection of lightning. The glow had been caused by the flare of a match.

He stood there watching expecting to see the light of a lamp which would tell him that Brent Wood or Jason Rudd had returned to work after hours; but the seconds passed and still the building remained dark. Not completely dark, though; the rear windows showed just a little less black than the ones near the front, so little that unless he had been looking for the difference he never would have detected it. There was just a little light in the bank, not more than would have been produced by, say, a dark lantern.

Jim's first thought was of burglars; his second, even more startling. Scotty had said that history repeats itself; was the one who had looted the bank the first time about to loot it again?

He turned into a passageway on his right and ran quickly to the alley. His spurs jingled as he ran and he stopped to bend over and remove them. Putting them into his pocket, he turned left and felt his way along the littered alley to the bank.

The windows were too high for him to look through, but the reflection of the light within was stronger. He stole up the bank steps, cautiously extended a hand towards where the doorknob should be. His fingers passed through an opening and his sleeve brushed the door frame. The door was open several inches!

Drawing his gun, Jim pushed slowly with his left hand. The door swung inward without a sound and he stepped over the sill and stood listening. He could hear nothing, and the open door was between him and the left side of the room. He took a cautious step forward and peered around its edge.

A thin beam of light close to the floor shone on a pair of boots and the dark front of the vault beyond. Nothing else was plain, but Jim was able after a moment to make out the vague form of a man, his shape almost blending with the shadows surrounding it.

He took one more step forward, then stopped as the man wheeled. The sound of a gasping breath reached him. He froze, his gun held rigidly before him, its hammer held back under a taut thumb, its muzzle pointed towards the fellow. Jim could not tell whether or not the other had a gun, but if he was a burglar it was almost a certainty that he had. For the space of five heartbeats the two stood facing each other, blind in the darkness; then from close to where the man's head must have been came a stab of flame and the crashing report of a six-gun, and by the light of the discharge Jim had a fleeting vision of a face with staring eyes and open mouth, a face upon which was written terror and awful apprehension.

Blackness came again, the more intense for the bright flash which had preceded it. There was a jar as a body struck the floor, the sharper sound of something falling near it.

Jim leaped forward, crashed violently into the tall stool which stood before the bookkeeping desk, and fell with it to the floor. The impact released his thumb hold on the hammer of his six-gun and the thunder of the report echoed through the building. He swore and struggled to his feet, kicking clear of the stool which had tripped him. Running to the vault he snatched up the dark lantern and flashed its beam on the stricken man. He had fallen backwards, had struck the door of the vault and then had collapsed in a heap on the floor. Beside him lay a gun, a thin eddy of smoke still coming from its muzzle.

The beam of light fell on the contorted face now rendered more hideous by the black hole in the forehead.

Randall's voice came in an awed half-whisper. "Dunham!"

On the surface the thing was plain. Lew Dunham was about to loot the bank; the stealth, the dark lantern, testified to that. But Dunham had heard Jim enter and, unable to see him in the darkness, knew that discovery or death was imminent. In the terror which followed realization, he had shot himself.

After the first shock, Jim's first thought was of his father. Would Dunham's act be accepted as an admission of guilt, a confirmation of Jim's belief that his father had been murdered by Dunham, or would the man, in destroying himself, have destroyed Jim's last chance of proving his father innocent of theft?

What he did then was perhaps the craziest thing he could have done. He turned and ran into Dunham's office, lighting his way with the lantern. He must have a look into Dunham's desk. If the man had kept the page he had cut from the tally book Jim would have not only the information it contained but also the strongest kind of evidence that it was Dunham who had not wanted him to see it. That in itself would be proof of Dunham's guilt.

He searched frantically, strewing the papers about recklessly, while the seconds ticked away. He finished the last drawer, turned despairingly towards the filing cabinets, then stopped as he caught a sound from the direction of the rear doorway. Quickly he closed the slide of the lantern. Somebody had come to investigate the shots; he'd wait until the fellow came inside, then slip from the office and through the outer doorway. He forgot for the moment that the glow from the lantern must have shown through the window of Dunham's office, forgot that others could tread just as softly as he had.

The light of another dark landern blazed directly into his face, blinding him. He tried to dodge out of its path.

"Hold it!" came Marshal Mosley's sharp voice. "Hold it, or I'll bust you plumb center! That's right. Now drop your gun and get your hands in the air. I reckon, Mister Randall, that there ain't no question of jurisdiction this time!"

Jim's gun clattered to the floor and he raised his hands above his head. There wasn't anything else he could do. He was trapped in the bank at midnight with Dunham dead on the floor and Dunham's papers scattered about him, and there were two shots that must be explained. The pound of boots in the alley told of the approach of more men.

"Maybe you'd better let me do some talking," Jim said tightly.

"You can do the talkin' later." Marshal Mosley raised his voice. "You, outside there! Come in here!"

A man felt his way into the dark bank. "What's up, Jeb?"

"Get some light in here."

A match flared and the man touched its flame to the wick of a lamp which stood on the bookkeeping desk.

"The big one now," directed Mosley without taking his eyes from Jim. "I want plenty of light."

The man righted the stool and climbed upon it, and a moment later the shadows dissolved under the rays of a big hanging lamp. Then, in the act of descending to the floor the fellow's gaze fell on the sprawled body in front of the safe and he came near to losing his balance. "Good gosh!" he gasped. "It's Lew Dunham, and dead as a cod!"

If the marshal was surprised he did not show it. "Come in here. Got a gun? Hold it on Randall and take this lantern. If he so much as winks, let him have it."

He waited until he was sure that Jim was not about to attempt a break then turned and strode to the vault. Several men had come through the doorway and were staring in dumb fascination. Jeb picked up the gun which lay near the dead man, threw out the cylinder and examined it briefly. Then he put it back where he found it, squeezed through the doorway into the office in such a way as not to come between Jim and the man who covered him, and picked up the gun Randall had dropped. Taking it out where the light was stronger he examined it also.

"Hm-m-m," he murmured, and looked at Jim. "Pretty plain, I reckon. Lew caught you here and you shot it out with him. He missed and you didn't."

"You got it all wrong. I was walking down the street and saw a light in the bank. The back door was open and I sneaked in. I found Lew in front of the vault with a dark lantern. My gun went off when I stumbled over the stool."

"Ain't that sad!" said Mosley sarcastically. "The bullet just accidentally hit Lew in the head."

"Not my bullet. Lew figured I'd caught him and shot himself."

"You'll have to think up a better one than that to tell the jury. They've already heard the one about the banker that got caught and committed suicide. Here, Slade; give me that lantern. And keep it shinin' on his face while you do it."

The exchange was made and now both of them had their Colts pointed at Jim. Mosley passed a pair of handcuffs to the other. "Get outside and slip these on Randall when he comes through the door." Slade slipped out of the small office and Mosley backed out after him, keeping light and gun trained on Jim. Clear of the doorway, the marshal said, "All right, Randall; you can come out now."

Had there been time to consider perhaps Jim would not have attempted what he did, so desperate it was, so almost certain to end in disaster. But there was no time to think and he acted almost involuntarily. He took three steps towards the entrance and found himself within reach of the edge of the door which projected into the office at a right angle to the wall. As his leg swung forward for the fourth step he kicked the door shut and leaped to one side.

The door closed with a violent bang which was immediately echoed by two more bangs from the outer room. Slugs tore through the wooden panels and thudded into the opposite wall; but Jim's leap had been in time and he was not hit.

Pausing just long enough to gather himself, Jim left the floor in a dive at the office window, head lowered, hands and wrists protecting the back of his neck. His head struck the sash squarely in the middle and wood and glass splintered as he went through. It was a six-foot drop to the ground and he landed with a jarring jolt, rolled to his feet and started on a wild run along the alley, stumbling over refuse, keeping his course by the line of the sky which showed above the roofs.

Behind him he left a medley of confused sounds and almost immediately there came the blast of six-guns. Lead whistled over his head and on both sides. He came to the end of the alley and stopped momentarily, peering desperately about him. A dark shape by the decrepit shed caught his attention and after a few quick steps the shape became that of a horse. With an exclamation of thankfulness Jim yanked the slipknot loose and leaped into the saddle. It was the horse Dunham had left there. He headed out over the range.

Presently he drew rein and heard the thud of pursuing hoofs. He changed course with the purpose of leading them in the wrong direction. After a while he altered the direction again, and when next he halted the sounds of pursuit had gone. Immediately he headed for the camp of his men, and his swift approach brought them to him at a run.

"You found out somethin'?" asked Tiny eagerly.

"I found out plenty! Was looking for Dirk when I saw a light inside the bank. The back door was open and I sneaked in. Somebody was monkeying with the safe; he heard me, got scared and shot himself before I could do a thing. It was Lew Dunham."

"Dunham! Great jumpin' Jerico!"

"Up to his old tricks, huh?" said Idaho Webb. "The low-down pup! Well, I reckon that settles things as far as you're concerned, Jim."

"You bet it does," said Jim bitterly. "Of all the fool luck! I started for him, of course, and had to fall over a stool and let my gun go off. Even then if I'd gone outside and yelled for help I would have been in the clear, but instead I had to run into Dunham's office to look for that missing page and Mosley found me there with Dunham's papers all over the floor. He figures that Lew caught me trying to rob the bank and that I killed him."

"Well—I'll—be!" exclaimed Sam Staley. "Jim, you sure manage to get into the dangdest messes! But if Mosley caught you, how come you're here? You shoot him, too?"

Jim told them of his desperate leap through the window and the finding of the horse.

"Your guardian angel sure has been workin' overtime," observed Scotty. "First you git caught breakin' into the Star and wiggle outa it, then you're caught in the bank with a fired gun and the vice-president dead on the floor and you wiggle out again. What's the next job you got cut out for yourself?"

"To find Linda. No matter what happens, that comes first."

"You're plumb wrong. The first thing to do is to start ridin' and keep ridin' until you're two hundred miles away. This yere thing ain't no petty breakin' and enterin'; it's murder, and you can bet your last chip there's a man high-tailin' it right now for Hartsville after the sheriff. He'll be here with a posse by noon tomorrow and he'll stay on the job till he finds you—or dies of old age tryin'."

"That's just why Linda must be found. The ones who have hidden her away know that if a search for me is started, they'll probably find her. And they'll be sure to see to it that she isn't found."

"You mean they'd *kill* her?" gasped Tiny.

"There's one who wouldn't draw the line at killing. Kidnapping a woman is a mighty serious offense, and if what she knows shows Dunham murdered my father, the one who did it will be shown to be hooked up with him and therefore just as guilty. If Linda doesn't know who kidnaped her, she'll be safe; but we can't afford to take a chance on that."

"Reckon you're right," admitted Scotty. "And they's another angle to the thing. If the evidence she gives shows Dunham up as a murderer, you won't be tried for killin' him. But I still think you oughta make yourself scarce and leave it to us to find the gal."

"Scotty, I can't leave. Not now. I'll find some place to hide." He thought swiftly, desperately. "I know one place where I'll be safe and where there's plenty of grub and water. I'll hide right on the Star."

Scotty stared at him. "You feel all right?"

"The Star's about the last place they'd look for me, isn't it? And I know every inch of the place. There a stable with a hayloft, and I can hide in the hay. Lane and his crew will be out hunting for Linda and I can help myself to grub. One of you can manage to hang around and watch the place. If you see a bit of rag in the loft window it'll mean that I want to get in touch with you."

They discussed it briefly but could think of no better arrangement; and Jim, after urging them to press the search for Linda, borrowed a gun from Sam Staley and rode away.

The Star bunkhouse was dark, but a light burned in the ranch house living room, and Jim could envision Alonzo Lane pacing up and down while he anxiously awaited news of his daughter. Jim circled the buildings and approached the stable from the rear. Near it was a carriage shed closed on three sides, and within this he tied his horse. It was a risk he must take; he might need the animal at a moment's notice.

Once in the loft, he made a nest in the hay into which he could crawl at the approach of danger; then he went to the little open window and looked out over the bunkhouse. And while they were still far away he heard the steady roll of hoofs.

The sound grew louder and presently Jim saw the ranch house door open as Lane came out to listen; then a light appeared in the bunkhouse and he heard the voices of the aroused men. A body of horsemen swept into the yard and Lane ran out to meet them. In a silence broken only by an occasional snort or stamp of a horse he caught bits of the conversation and knew that Mosley was talking of the death of Lew Dunham.

He heard Lane tell of Linda's disappearance and Mosley's assurance that they would look for her too; he heard Jeff Dirk's voice as he urged the marshal and his party to spend the night at the Star. Then came five minutes of orderly confusion while horses were off-saddled and corralled and men trooped into the house and the crew's quarters. All except the light in the ranch house living room were extinguished and again there fell silence.

Jim remained at the window watching while the stars brightened and then paled and the dark pall in the east was pushed back by a slowly rising sun. If Dirk had abducted Linda, as Jim believed, Jeff might take this opportunity of warning Linda's guards that the search was on. But men stirred and lamps were lighted, and smoke came from the stack of the mess shack and no one had left the ranch.

Breakfast was eaten while it was still dark, and the figures of men and horses were just discernible when they rode away towards the hills. The marshal's party left first; Dirk and the Star men, Alonzo Lane with them, followed at a distance of several hundred yards.

Certain that all had departed but the cook and that he would be busy with the dishes, Jim descended from the loft, went to his horse and, quickly saddling, set out on the heels of Dirk's men. The blood was pounding in his veins, not alone from excitement but also with the knowledge that if Dirk had abducted Linda he would find some way of contacting the ones who held her prisoner this very day.

It was easy to follow them by the sounds they made. They rode in a westerly direction, evidently intending to start at the beginning of the range of hills and work eastward. The light grew stronger, but by the time the sun appeared Jim was safely among the trees at the base of the hills. Here he halted and when he failed to hear the sound of movement ahead of him decided that Dirk's men had also stopped.

He waited, keeping a sharp lookout, and then heard them resume their way, angling higher into the hills. He followed cautiously until the trampled earth told him that it was here where they had stopped. He rode a bit farther, saw where the main body of riders had turned to the right, saw some broken brush where a single one of them had continued westward. Face tight, he followed this trail, guessing that Dirk had found an excuse for leaving the party and would head for the place where Linda was being held.

His guess as to the rider's identity was confirmed a little later when the horseman crossed an open space. It was Dirk, all right. Jim waited at the edge of the clearing until it was safe to proceed. The hills were curving to the south now, and Dirk followed their contour until at last Jim saw a little shack in a hollow at the extreme western limit of the Star range and knew it for one of their line camps.

When he pulled to a walk he could no longer hear Jeff's horse, so for five minutes he let his mount pick its way then slipped to the earth, tethered the animal, and went ahead on foot. Presently he heard a whistle and, looking, through the screen of trees, saw a man come out of the shack, look about him, then start towards the slope behind the cabin.

Swiftly Jim stole through the trees, working towards the point for which the man was headed. He lost sight of him almost at once, but continued on with the caution of a stalking Indian. And at last he heard voices.

They were quite close, just under the lip of a little gully not more than twenty feet beyond him, and for a moment he was tempted to risk jumping them. Better judgment prevailed; they would be sure to hear him approach and in their present mood would not hesitate to kill him if they could. That would end his chance to save Linda. He backed softly away, circled and went down to a place where he could see the cabin.

There was another man in sight now. He sat on a bench in front of the shack with a Winchester rifle standing within easy reach. Presently the man who had gone to meet Dirk came swinging into sight; he spoke to the other and went into the cabin. Behind him, Jim heard the sounds of Dirk's departure, and after a few seconds he knew that Dirk was heading in the opposite direction, following the curve of the hills on the shortest route to Briscoe.

Randall withdrew to the place where he had left his horse, his mind busy with his problem. He made his decision quickly. It was broad daylight, but the posse would be searching the hills and would not expect to find him on the open range. He rode boldly out into the valley and headed straight for the Star.

CHAPTER NINE

JIM REACHED the Star without mishap to find it utterly deserted, the cook having gone to Briscoe to gather the news. Leading his horse into the carriage shed, Jim loosened the cinches and slipped the bit, tying the animal by a neck halter in the darkest corner. Then he helped himself to a measure of grain and a bucket of water and placed them within reach of the horse.

He was anxious to get in touch with his men, but seeking them out directly was out of the question. He had tempted fate far enough as it was. He went up into the loft, took the scarf from about his neck and draped it over the window sill so that one corner hung outside, then settled himself to wait.

After what seemed hours he heard the thud of hoofs and saw Juan ride into sight. The Mexican gave no indication of having seen the signal, riding directly to the ranch house and knocking on the door. Receiving no answer, he went to the mess shack and looked inside, then visited the bunkhouse. Jim was standing just within the stable doorway when he rounded the building.

"Where are the boys?" he asked when Juan had joined him.

"At the camp to eat the dinner. All the tam we look and find nossing." Juan shrugged desparingly. "Ees lak look for needle in the smokestack."

"Bring them here as quick as you can. I know where Linda is and I'm hoping they won't move her before we get there."

Juan exclaimed his amazement and Jim told him how he had followed Dirk to the line cabin at the west end of the Star range. "I'll wait for you here and we'll ride after her. Hurry!"

Juan left at a high lope and Jim went back to his window. The minutes dragged and he feared that Dirk might bring his crew in for dinner, but at last his boys came sweeping over the rise and he went down to prepare his horse. Wisely they rode into the Star yard and scattered as though to search the buildings, thus making it possible for Jim to join them without attracting the attention of anyone who might be watching from the hills. They set out across the range at a swinging lope, keeping closely bunched so as to shield Randall from observation.

"This is plumb crazy," said Sam Staley. "You're fixin' to run your neck straight into a noose, comin' with us. We know where that line shack is; we could get her without you,"

"Got to chance it, Sam. I'm staking everything on what Linda found in that tally book."

"Here's a telegram Scotty just fetched from town," said Idaho Webb, and passed over the slip of yellow paper. "It sounds right interestin'."

Jim read the written form as he rode. It said,

LAWYER YOU NAME HAS SHADY REPUTATION. HIS BANK CLERK BROTHER ABSCONDED TWO YEARS AGO WITH TEN THOUSAND. AM CHECKING AND WILL FORWARD DESCRIPTION OF BROTHER AS SOON AS I CAN GET IT.

The message was from the detective Jim had hired.

"So the Acme lawyer has a brother who ran away with ten thousand bucks," commented Sam. "And your detective feller figures the description is goin' to fit somebody at this end of the line."

"I'm betting it will, too. And I think I know who that somebody is. If I'm right, that noose Sam mentioned will never fit my neck! Two years ago; that's about the time Lew Dunham drifted into Briscoe, isn't it?"

"That's right."

When they had ridden for two hours the hills on both sides of the valley began to close in to form the pocket in which was tucked the Star line cabin. The posse was in these hills and their nearness spelled increased danger.

Randall paid it no attention. He was in it now, and he would not back out. "We'll pull up here and go on at a trot. I'll circle the hollow where the cabin is so as to come at them from the rear in case they start something. You boys ride straight to the shack. Tell anybody you find there that you're hunting for Linda Lane and want something to eat."

He left them and trotted around the ridge which cut off their view of the cabin, while they continued straight over its crest. Beyond the fringe of trees he dismounted and threaded his way through the brush, leading the horse. He came to a faint trail which angled down the slope and, following it, presently sighted the cabin. There were three horses in the little corral and he could see the four belonging to his men standing over trailing reins before the shack. There was no indication of any disturbance within the cabin or outside it, and no sound reached him. Either his boys had earned a bloodless victory or Linda was not here after all.

He frowned apprehensively. Linda must be here. She had to be here.

At the rear corner of the cabin he dropped the rein. Voices reached him now, pitched at the level of ordinary conversation. He swung around to the front of the cabin and stepped through the open doorway.

A single sweeping glance took in the whole interior. Two bunks, stove, table, a cupboard fashioned from a dry-goods box, a couple of broken chairs, a dirty rag rug on the floor beneath the table. His own boys were standing around munching food which had been hurriedly supplied; the three Star men, Panhandle's former buddies, watched them suspiciously. As Jim entered, these three made hostile motions toward their guns but halted as his own Colt swept up.

He said, "Not here?" and his voice was sharp with disappointment.

"Not here," answered Tiny grimly.

"Who ain't here?" growled one of the Star men.

"Linda Lane. She was here; what did you do with her?"

"You're loco. Ain't seen her since yesterday."

Jim walked around the room peering beneath the bunks and looking behind the stove while they watched in scornful amusement. There was no place within the single room where she could be hidden. Jim holstered his gun and started for the door. "Let's go," he said dejectedly.

And then he stopped abruptly and turned. His men turned also and the three from the Star seemed to tense. From somewhere within the cabin had come a muffled thump!

Jim stood like a pointing hound trying to locate the direction of the sound. There was a moment of tense silence, then it came again. And this time Jim located the source. He leaped for the table, thrust it aside.

"No you don't!" shrilled one of the Star men, and went for his gun.

Randall tipped the heavy table and dropped behind it as the fellow's Colt roared. The slug bored through the table and grazed his neck. He dropped flat on the floor, yanked his own six-gun. Behind him another Colt thundered and he heard Juan's jubilant shout, "I get heem!" Then came a crashing crescendo of sound and lead bored through the air above Jim.

He worked to the end of the table and peered around it, his gun extended before him. Two of the Star men were down; the third had ducked behind the stove and had his gun levelled over it.

"Get that louse!" came Sam's shout. "Get him or—"

Jim could see only the exposed left foot of the kneeling man. He put a slug into it and the fellow jerked erect, howling with pain. It was his undoing; four bullets crashed into his head and the howl died like that of a strangled dog.

Randall got to his feet and looked about him. Idaho Webb was leaning against the wall, his face white, a hand pressed to his shoulder; Tiny was dabbing at his head with a bloody scarf; Sam and Juan appeared to be uninjured. The room was blue with powder smoke. At the back of the cabin sprawled the Star men. The whole thing had happened in a space of ten seconds.

"The danged fools," said Sam. "They didn't have a chance."

"They knew the goose ees cook'," observed Juan. "I'm sorry the senor Dirk ees not 'ere. I'm still weesh to see heem keek!"

"How bad you hurt, Idaho?"

"Shoulder. Busted my collar bone, likely." Idaho grinned a sickly grin. "I ain't gonna die by a long shot."

"That jigger behind the stove parted my hair," complained Tiny, "and ruined a forty-dollar hat while he was doin' it. The skunk! Say, Jim, if we don't find her now we'll all of us wind up with our necks in that noose!"

Jim pushed the table aside and kicked back the rag rug. Beneath it he found a trapdoor. He grasped a nail and pulled and it came away, revealing a hole not more than four feet square and half as deep. Squeezed into this space, bound securely and with a gag in her mouth, was Linda.

Tenderly he lifted her out and carried her to one of the bunks; swiftly Juan's knife freed her.

"Linda, darling, are you all right?"

"Yes." She looked past him at the huddled bodies on the floor and shuddered. "Oh!" she cried, and buried her face in her hands.

Jim seated himself beside her, put his arms about her and held her close. He nodded towards the bodies, then towards the door. Juan and Sam and Tiny each picked up a Star man and carried him from the room.

Linda was trembling and sobbing softly. Jim held her, remembering how she had clung to his hand in his hour of pain. Sam and Juan got water and a clean flour sack and went to work on Tiny and Idaho. The minutes passed.

Presently the sobs ceased and Linda looked up at Jim. "I'm—all right now," she said.

He removed his arms. "Atta girl! You're sure a soldier, Linda."

"I'm not. I'm a coward, Jim. I was so afraid!" She was quiet for a moment and he took her hand in his. Presently she went on. "They did it to keep me from telling you, of course. I was on my way to your place. It was still light and I was half way there. They rode out from beside the trail and one of them grabbed the rein and stopped me. I hit him with my quirt but he just grinned at me. When I tried to slip out of the saddle another one grabbed me and held me—like a sack of bran. They rode into the woods and after a while one of them brought up my horse and they put me into the saddle and tied me there. By this time I knew they had kidnapped me to keep me from telling you what I'd read in your father's tally book. Jim it said—"

"Never mind just now; tell me what happened to you."

"That's all. They brought me here and tied my feet and told me that if I yelled they'd put a gag in my mouth. Last night they gave me a blanket but I couldn't sleep. They took turns watching. This morning they fixed some breakfast for me; then somebody whistled and one of them went out to meet him. When he came back he acted excited. I heard him tell the others that you had shot Mr. Dunham. Jim, you didn't, did you?"

"No. Was Jeff Dirk with these men at any time?"

"Jeff? Of course not. Well, right after that they tied me hand and foot and made a gag, and they pulled the table aside and opened the trapdoor. They intended putting me in there if the sheriff came here in search of you. One of them stayed outside all the time to keep watch and the others kept near me. When they saw your boys coming they slipped the gag into my mouth and pushed me down there and closed the trapdoor. I thought I'd smother. When I heard your voice I signaled by bumping my head against the trapdoor. Thank goodness you heard me!"

There was a moment of silence, then Jim spoke. It was an effort to keep his voice steady. "And now—the tally book."

"Oh, yes! Jim, that night you gave it to me I sat by the window thinking about it, and the more I thought the more I realized just how much it meant to you. If by any chance it did prove that your father was no thief and no suicide, I knew whoever was guilty would do everything to get it before you could read it. And so I read it myself, every word of it."

They were all gathered about her now, listening avidly. Jim said, "You did right, Linda. Go on."

"You know what was in that book, all except that last page. You know there were no large investments, no big losses. And then, on the very last page, I came to an entry which I saw was the key to the whole thing. It was written a day or so before your father's death. It said—I memorized it—'Tomorrow Rudd will finish his audit. I don't know what he will find, but at the most I've advanced five thousand dollars without security. And they won't let me pay it off in cash. No, sir! In accordance with banking procedure I must give my note, secured by a mortgage on the Star. I'm sorry I ever got into the banking business where a man's word is no good.'"

She looked up at Jim. His eyes were bright and his face had tightened. "You see the significance of that entry?"

"See it! I should say I do! Dad says the amount was five thousand dollars, and the note and mortgage—"

He broke off abruptly at the sound of footsteps outside the cabin. Men stood in the doorway, grim men holding guns which covered him and his men. One of them was Jeff Dirk and another was the sheriff from Hartsville. The latter spoke. "Up with 'em, all of you! No monkey business. Jim Randall, you're under arrest for the murder of Lewis Dunham."

Jim Randall spoke quietly. "Don't touch your guns, boys." He set the example by getting to his feet and raising his hands. "Come in, Sheriff; you're the very man I want to see."

"Well, that's interestin'," said the sheriff drily. "Especially since it looks like there'll be a charge of kidnapin' against you in addition to murder."

"He didn't kidnap me," explained Linda. "It was those men—outside. They tied my hands and feet and gagged me and squeezed me under that trapdoor when Jim and his men came to look for me."

"And the leader of them," added Jim, "is Jeff Dirk, right there beside you."

Dirk appeared astonished. "Me? Why, the man's crazy! I was at the ranch the whole time. Linda can tell you that I had nothing to do with it."

"Jeff wasn't with them at any time," she confirmed.

"Well, that clears up the kidnapin'," the sheriff stated. "The three that done it are dead. Which still leaves the murder charge against you, Randall. Ed, take his gun and put the cuffs on him."

"You can have my gun and welcome, but there's a lot to explain. If you'll give me about ten minutes I think I can make you change your mind about the cuffs."

"You can do all the talkin' you want to later on."

"Please let him explain," begged Linda. "You see my kidnaping wasn't just an accident or an attempt to collect ransom; the men were hired to get me out of the way so that I couldn't give Jim some information I had that might lead to the clearing of his father. It won't take long to hear what he has to say."

"It'll take too long to suit me," snapped Dirk. "Go on, Ed; put the cuffs on him."

His assumption of authority irked the sheriff. "Hold your hosses, Dirk; I'm runnin' this show. Ed, take the guns. You fellows line up against the wall. Keep them covered, boys."

When the guns had been collected, the sheriff came into the room and seated himself a short distance from Jim and Linda, who had returned to their places on the edge of the bunk. Jim's four cowboys stood against the wall, the sheriff's men watching them alertly. Jeff Dirk stood leaning against the door frame, scowling.

"Now," said the sheriff, "make it fast. And remember that anything you say can be used in evidence against you."

So Jim told him everything, starting with the summons which brought him from Montana and the attempts on his life on the way south. Linda corroborated his story of the attack in Cottonwood Junction and the sheriff was properly impressed. He told of the later efforts to get him out of Briscoe. "I thought at first that Lew Dunham wanted to get rid of me so he could have my homestead; later I decided that he didn't want me around because I might get curious about my father's death."

"Dunham had nothin' to do with that," stated the sheriff flatly. "I investigated that angle myself."

"But there were some things you didn't find out, couldn't find out."

He told of the bit of burned picture and the significance it held; told of the failure to locate the officers of the Acme Cattle Company; showed the sheriff the telegram which stamped the Acme lawyer a shady character and the brother of a thieving bank clerk; told of the hidden tally book and the page which was cut from it after it had been placed in Dunham's keeping; related the events which culminated in the shooting of Dunham. And as he talked, the skepticism on the sheriff's face changed slowly to wonder and then deep interest. He leaned forward in his chair, and his men forgot their vigilance. Nobody noticed when Jeff Dirk slipped quietly from the doorway and tip-toed away. No one noticed the soft pad of hoofs that told of his stealthy departure.

"You sure are givin' me a different picture of the whole thing," admitted the sheriff. "What did that missin' page say to bear out your hunch that John Randall didn't rob the bank and then commit suicide?"

"It said that as near as he could estimate it, the amount he owed the bank was around five thousand dollars. *Five* thousand, not *fifty*."

"Hm-m-m. Then why did he turn right around and sign a note and a mortgage for fifty thousand? If he was in his right mind he certainly wouldn't have done that unless he knew he really owed it."

Jim was working at the lining of his coat, his fingers trembling a bit with excitement. "You're right; he never would have signed for that amount. I have the note and mortgage right here; never checked them over for anything but the signatures, and they're genuine enough. Now—" He drew forth the papers, smoothed them out, looked carefully at the amount on the note then held it so that the light struck the surface of the paper at an angle. Linda, looking over his shoulder, gave a little exclamation and Jim handed the note to the sheriff with a grim, "Look at it against the light."

The sheriff did so. "Erased, by the Lord Harry! A neat job, but the word 'five' has been changed to 'fifty' and another cipher added to the figures."

Jim and Linda were examining the mortgage. "It's been changed here, too. Neatly, and it never would have been questioned. It never was questioned. Sheriff, the amount was five thousand when my father signed and Brent Wood witnessed the signature, but it was raised later. But to make it stand up my father had to die. He was shot as he sat at his desk, shot with his own gun and at close range so that it would look like suicide. When he was dead the bank was cleaned out to the tune of another twenty thousand, which theft would naturally be blamed on him!"

The sheriff was convinced now. "That note has sure enough been changed, and so has the mortgage. And the telegram makes it look like the Acme Cattle Company is just a blind. Miss Lane, has your father ever dealt direct with the Acme people?"

"No. Always through their lawyer. It was the lawyer who called at the very beginning to offer my father the managership of the ranch, and all father's records are sent to him."

"See how it fits?" cried Jim. "Lew Dunham comes out here two years ago, an absconding bank clerk, and uses the stolen money to stock the Bar D. After he is established he persuades my father to open the bank and at the first opportunity gets him to give his note and mortgage for five thousand dollars. Lew raises the amount to fifty thousand and—and—" He faltered to a stop, a puzzled look crossing his face. Quite suddenly he had run into an obstacle, an obstacle which could not be surmounted.

"Go ahead," said the sheriff. "Lew shoots your father and helps himself to some seventy thousand dollars. He buys the Star, usin' the Acme Cattle Company as a blind, the deal bein' completed through his lawyer brother. Boy, that's the biggest steal I ever heard of, and it all makes sense."

"No," said Jim puzzledly. "No, it doesn't." He passed a hand over his brow and sat down on the bunk again. His voice was weak, shaken.

"What do you mean? You got the whole thing figured out so that a blind man could see it, and now you say it don't make sense."

"That's right. It was done the way I told you but it couldn't have been Lew Dunham who did it."

"Why not? It was Lew who got your father to start the bank, Lew who talked him into signin' that note and givin' the mortgage, Lew who waited two months before sendin' for you, Lew who wanted you out of the way so's he could have the homestead. Why wasn't it Lew?"

"For lots of reasons I can think of now. If it had been Lew, he'd never have sent for me in the first place. And if he had, he'd have treated me differently when I got here. It wouldn't have cost him a thing to be sympathetic and friendly instead of cold and hostile." Jim was warming to the subject as the shock of discovery wore of. "I never could quite figure him out; now I know that he really thought my father guilty. He swore that he was up at the Argosy mine the night my father was killed; we checked up on the story and the mind superintendent backed him up. Nobody saw him in Briscoe that afternoon or night. But the main reason why I'm sure he didn't do it is that he didn't see that note and mortgage until *after the amounts had been changed.*"

They were staring at him, still not fully understanding.

"Don't you see?" Jim was on his feet again. "The amount was five thousand dollars when Dad signed. He was killed shortly after he signed, that same evening, anyhow. Immediately after his death it was found that the note and mortgage were for fifty thousand dollars. But all that time Lew was at the Argosy mine."

"Yeah," said the sheriff slowly, "I see. But if it wasn't Dunham, who was it?"

"The one who kept reminding Dunham of the shortage, of the difficulty of keeping the books straight. The man who made the audit, who found an additional twenty thousand gone after my father's death. He's the man who murdered my father. *Jason Rudd!*"

"Oh, no!" cried Linda. "It couldn't be! He's such a harmless, friendly little man!"

"As harmless and friendly as a coral snake!"

"Sure looks like you got him pinned," said the sheriff. "But Lew could have been in it with him. There's that tally sheet, you know."

"Lew put it in the vault where Rudd could get at it easily enough. And Lew was really mad when I accused him of cutting out that page. No, it was Rudd and Rudd alone. Dirk worked for him, not for Lew; but when he wanted to make a report to Rudd in a hurry he went to Lew—talking loud enough for Rudd to hear what he said. Oh, they were slick!"

"Dirk!" snapped the sheriff, and turned to look at the door-way where Jeff had been standing. "Where is he?"

But Dirk was gone. A posseman went outside, looked around, came back and reported. "Hoss gone and nowhere in sight. He's hightailed it."

"He won't get far. Randall, I guess you got things figured out right at last. The county'll reopen the case and there's no doubt in my mind that your father'll be completely cleared. As for you—well, it's just too bad that you didn't let the blame rest on Dunham, as far as you're concerned. You shot a little too soon. That murder charge will stick now."

"But I didn't shoot Lew, I tell you."

"Then who did? After provin' him innocent you can't make me believe he shot himself."

"I don't believe he did—now. Sheriff, he was shot by the same man who shot my father. By Rudd. It has to be that way. Remember, I was in the dark and couldn't see a thing except a little of Dunham's legs and the lower part of the safe. That shot came from close to where Lew's head must have been, but that doesn't mean that Lew fired the shot."

"You mean Rudd was in the bank too—? And shot him?"

"What," said Linda suddenly, "was Mr. Dunham doing prowling about in the bank with a dark lantern? Isn't it just possible that he went there to check up on Rudd? He knew that a page had been cut out of the tally book and he knew that he hadn't cut it out. There were only two others who could have done it, Brent Wood or Jason Rudd. He didn't want them to know—"

"That's it!" cried Jim. "Listen! Suppose that missing page made Lew suspicious of Rudd. Suppose he sneaked into the bank to check up on the money in the vault or to look for that missing page. He'd have locked the door after him, wouldn't he? Sure he would! Yet when I went in *the door was open*! Why? Because Jason Rudd had seen the light too and had unlocked the door after him and followed him in! It was Rudd who left the door open. I'm positive I didn't make a sound, yet Lew suddenly wheeled when he heard somebody near him move.

"Then came the shot that killed him. From right close, so it would look like suicide. Don't you see? Rudd followed him in and saw his chance. If he was caught he could swear that he'd caught Lew rifling the vault and had shot him as a burglar. Or he could say that Lew shot himself when Rudd challenged him. Either way Rudd was safe, could loot the bank of more money and have it blamed on Dunham. Just as he had it blamed on my father before."

"Now," said the sheriff, "the picture's gettin' plain again. Rudd didn't know you were there, but when you tripped over the stool he knew somebody had seen and heard that shot and got out of there in a hurry. Whoever it was would be found with Dunham's dead body and would have to do the explainin'. He must have been right tickled when he found it was you. Lew was dead and you would be hanged for his murder. But there was still Miss Lane with her knowledge of the contents of that missin' page, and so he used Dirk—" He broke off. "All theory, of course; but the proof'll come now that we know what to look for. And when the description of the missin' bank clerk arrives we'll clamp down on Jason Rudd. No need to hurry it; as long as he doesn't know we suspect him—"

"You're forgetting Dirk," interrupted Jim. "I don't know how much he heard, but it must have been enough to tip him off."

The sheriff sprang to his feet. "By George, that's right! Hit leather, boys! Randall, I'm releasin' you in the custody of—of—Miss Lane, there."

There was a scramble for horses. Jim's cowboys recovered their guns and went outside with the possemen. Randall spoke to Idaho Webb. "You stay here and take it easy. I'll send the doc out to set that collar bone. Miss Lane, I'll catch up a hoss for you and you can head for the Star. Your father'll be glad to know you're safe."

"My father," she said quietly, "is probably in the hills looking for me. I've got to see this thing through. Jim, I'm going with you."

The sheriff frowned. "I'd rather you didn't, ma'am."

"But I have to. Jim's in my custody, you know."

Jim smiled and rested a hand on her shoulder. "Sure you're going along. You can ride one of the Star horses."

They went out to the corral together.

CHAPTER TEN

JEFF DIRK rapped softly on the back door, two wide-spaced raps, two quick ones. It was quite dark, for the line camp was at the extreme end of the basin and fully half the distance to Briscoe was over hilly, broken terrain. Close by a blob of deeper black in the darkness showed the location of his wet horse. It stood with lowered head, heaving.

The door opened and Dirk slipped inside. Jason Rudd shot the bolt and wheeled to face him. "Well?"

There was nothing now in Rudd's attitude that would suggest the meek, harmless bookkeeper. The eyes which regarded Dirk through the thick-lensed glasses were sharp, the lines of his face harsh, the thin lips drawn back in a somewhat wolfish snarl.

"We're through," answered Dirk shortly. "The deal's down to the last card and our luck's run out."

"They found the girl?"

"Yes. Randall and his men."

"Randall! And you let him get away with it? You missed another chance to finish him? Oh, you fool!"

Dirk's face darkened. "Easy with that kind of talk! I'm done taking lip from you. My men had her tied and gagged and stuffed in that hole under the floor when Randall's bunch rode up. To start shooting on sight would have been a dead give-away. Randall searched the place and started off, but Linda attracted his attention by bumping her head on the trapdoor. Hell broke loose then. Schwingle, Lafe, Bill—all three of them—were killed. I had just met the sheriff's party working west through the hills.

We heard the shooting and went to the cabin. Randall was nailed all right, but the girl persuaded the sheriff to let him talk and the last I heard they were having a regular experience meeting. I got away from there while I could."

"They've got nothing on me, nothing at all. Nothing but Randall's claim that the mortgage was for five thousand instead of fifty. And that comes at second-hand, through the girl."

"Yeah? How you going to explain the erasures on the note and mortgage?"

"Erasures?" Rudd was stumped for a moment. "Merely an error in making out the amount, corrected."

"Swell—except that the 'correction' was made by a defaulting cashier from a Philadelphia bank. Yes, they know that. Randall's had a detective working on the case; he checked up on your lawyer brother and a description of the defaulting cashier is on its way."

Rudd's face was livid. "You've bungled it, Dirk; bungled it from the very start. You sent that dodo of a Panhandle and his brother to waylay Randall. The brother got killed and Panhandle has to run for it like a licked pup. Your whole bunch got him alone at the homestead and instead of putting a slug through his head and planting him, they let him come back and tie them up like turkeys. Panhandle dumps him into a mine shaft without first making sure he's dead, and he comes back and shoots Panhandle! He even socks you on the chin and—" He broke off to stamp furiously across the room and back. "Now," he went on, "we're in it. Up to our necks."

"You weren't so smart yourself," answered Dirk angrily. "Why didn't you start a fire in that safe and burn the whole tally book instead of cutting out a page? That gave away the whole play. Dunham guessed that you'd done it and you had to kill him. Why didn't you sit tight and let him and Randall shoot it out?"

"I didn't know Randall was in the bank or I'd have saved the bullet for him. It all comes back on you, Jeff. I told you to get rid of Randall; you should have attended to it yourself. You didn't because you were afraid of getting in bad with Linda."

"Don't fool yourself, Jas. It wasn't Linda that stopped me, it was you. I wasn't sticking my neck out too far on your account. You murdered John Randall, the best friend you ever had. You murdered Lew Dunham, who trusted you and believed in you. You'd murder me just as quick if you thought you could pick up an extra nickle by it."

The look Rudd gave him was venomous. "Maybe I would if I had time. I haven't. Neither have you. We're both in it and we've got to slope before Randall and the sheriff figure out the whole play. You know the way to the Border?"

"Yes."

"Get two good horses; I'll put up some grub."

"Just a minute, Jas. From here on we work together. I'll help you put up the grub and I'll go with you to clean out the bank. We'll split fifty-fifty, the money in the vault and what you've salted away here. Then I'll get the horses."

"Fifty-fifty! You're crazy! You're working for a salary. I'll give you a bonus of a thousand."

The sneer was back on Dirk's lips. "Listen, you little rat! Ever hear of an accessory before and after the fact? Well, that's me. But there's one good thing about being an accessory, I can turn you in and get off myself. I want half of that *dinero,* right down to the last cent."

Rudd glared at him in speechless rage. Had he dared he would have drawn the derringer under his arm and shot him; but he knew that at the slightest suspicious move Dirk would pull his big Colt and kill him. And receive the thanks of the community for doing so. The fire in his eyes died, the taut muscles relaxed. "All right, Jeff," he said quietly. "Fifty-fifty."

They went about gathering food to last them on their short dash to the Border, each pretending perfect confidence in the other, each ready for action at the first suspicious move by his companion. They made two parcels of it, then Rudd removed a floor board and took from the opening packet after packet of banknotes.

"Better than gold," he explained tersely. "Easier to carry. I kept changing it a little at a time."

The money was divided and each man placed his share in the sack with his provisions. They went to the door together.

"After you," said Jeff politely, and Rudd stepped over the sill without hesitancy. Dirk joined him and they stood looking about them for a moment then crossed the street and made their way to the alley on the other side. Along it they moved, Jeff close on the heels of Rudd, until they reached the bank. Rudd fitted a key in the lock and they entered the building.

"Keep your back to me," warned Dirk, and placed a hand on Rudd's shoulder.

"We'll need a light," said Jason. "I must see to work the combination."

"Light a lamp, then. Nobody in town to interfere."

Rudd moved to the bookkeeping desk with Dirk still behind him and quickly lighted the lamp which stood there. He turned the wick low.

"Now," said Dirk, "take that derringer out from under your arm and put it in a drawer of the desk."

Slowly Rudd turned. "You're asking just a bit too much. If I give up my gun, you'll do the same."

Dick regarded him for a moment, considering the matter. He intended to kill the little man, of course, but the killing must be postponed until he had access to the money in the safe. And after all, this insignificant person would be harmless without a gun.

"Right," he said and drew open a drawer. "We'll stand side by side and both shuck 'em at the same time."

They drew their guns. Jeff watched his companion closely, prepared to turn slow motion into a blur of action at the least suspicious move; but Rudd kept the gun pointed away from Dirk and the two weapons were deposited side by side. Gently Rudd pushed the drawer shut.

"Now for the cleanup," he said. "You hold the light."

Dirk had the sack of grub and loot in his left hand; he could feel the comfortable pressure of the gun under his arm and smiled that little twisted smile of his. Rudd, poor fool, did not suspect that he was still armed. After the safe was opened—!

Rudd moved confidently to the vault and Dirk stationed himself where the light from the lamp which Dirk held would fall on the dials. Quickly Rudd worked, the mechanism clicked, he twirled the locking wheels. The heavy doors were drawn open.

"Some of it is here," said the little bookkeeper. "The rest is inside the inner safe." He knelt on the floor, Dirk crouching behind him holding the lamp. It's feeble rays did not penetrate far into the gloomy interior. Rudd chuckled. "There's a special package I hid in this pigenhole," he said over his shoulder. "One that I kept for just such an emergency." His hand probed the recess. "Ah! Here it is. Hold your sack, Jeff."

Dirk put the sack on the floor and let it fall open. Awkwardly he got hold of the cloth with two of the fingers which held the lamp. With his left hand he spread the opening wide, leaning over to receive the bundle of banknotes which he expected Rudd to hand him.

But it wasn't a package of notes that Rudd held. Jeff saw it as Rudd turned and a gasp of sudden chilling apprehension forced itself from his lips. He didn't have a chance; there were too many moves to make. He pulled up his left hand and quickly shifted the lamp into it, then his right hand darted beneath his coat. But Rudd was chuckling up at him and his tense fingers never reached the derringer which was hidden there.

He saw the mocking light in Rudd's eyes through the thick glass which covered them, saw the wolfish grin on the thin lips. It was his last look upon the living. The heavy Colt in Rudd's hand roared, its report deafening in the confines of the building.

Dirk rocked backwards, the lamp in his left hand tilting. Quickly Rudd reached out and plucked the lamp away.

"Mustn't let it fall," he said softly. "You might start a fire."

Dirk slumped slowly forward and Rudd fended off the body with his gun so that it would not topple against him.

Ears still ringing from the report, he started gathering up the money about him. The air was foul from powder fumes and he went outside for a moment for a clean breath. And then he heard a sound which froze him in his tracks.

What he heard was the thud of many hoofs in the street.

The sheriff halted his party at the end of the street to give them their instructions. "We'll go afoot from here on, leavin' a man with the hosses. Miss Lane, you'll stay with him. Randall, you and your three take one side of the street, the rest of us will take the other. One man in each party will move along the alley to stop anybody that's got ideas about slippin' out of town and warnin' the two we want. Don't let anybody leave until—"

He broke off abruptly. From somewhere down the street had come the sullen, muffled report of a gun. Under ordinary conditions the report of a firearm held little significance in a town like Briscoe; but now, under the strain of the climax which each felt was approaching, it held them in a momentary grip of silence and apprehension. In the next instant they were riding in a body towards the place from whence the shot had come.

Men came pouring out of the saloons, attracted not so much by the shot as by the flurry of hoofbeats which followed it. They ran along the sidewalks, and the sheriff, reining in momentarily, called, "Where did that shot come from?"

Nobody knew. Then Jim spoke sharply. "There's a light in the bank!"

They spurred to the squat brick building and flung themselves from their horses.

"Kelly," ordered the sheriff sharply, "you and Arch watch the front. The rest of us'll take the back." He ran for the passageway which ran between the bank and the adjacent building. Jim and his boys were already racing along it towards the alley.

They rounded the rear corner of the building and ran towards the open rear doorway, through which a faint shaft of light penetrated the blackness of the alley. The sheriff caught up with them and ran up the low steps, Jim beside him. They kicked the door wide and leaped into the bank, their eyes stabbing the shadows.

A lamp, wick turned low, burned on the bookkeeper's desk, intensifying the gloom in the farther reaches of the banking room. A faint odor of burned power lingered in the air, but there was no sound, no movement. The doors of the big vault were closed.

"Something on the floor over there by the safe," said Jim.

"Follow close," ordered the sheriff over his shoulder. "One of you fellers stay at the door."

Warily they advanced, eyes probing, ears alert, guns extended before them. Jim reached the desk and turned the lamp wick high. The sheriff walked over to the body on the floor. It was lying face down. He raised the head, then lowered it again."

"It's Dirk," he said flatly.

"And through the head," murmured Jim. "Like Lew Dunham—and Dad."

"You fellers spread out and look around. Ben, you and Art take the offices; you Star men, get out there in the lobby. Miss Lane, what you doin' here? Go over there behind the safe."

The search was swift and thorough; there were few hiding places inside the building and all of them were empty.

"He's gone," said the sheriff when all had reported. "We'll search the town first. Randall, you stay here with Miss Lane. It's too risky for her to go rammin' around in the dark with a killer on the loose. Just lay low and keep your gun on the door. I'll leave it open. If he comes in, get the drop on him, and if you have to shoot, shoot quick."

He hurried from the room, the others at his heels. Jim and Linda heard the crunch of their boots as they trod the passageway to the street. He was standing by the bookkeeping desk and she came over to join him. "I guess that description of the missing bank clerk isn't necessary now," she said. "Jim, how did it happen? To Jeff, I mean."

He looked at the huddled figure on the floor and shook his head. "We can only guess. Jeff rode in to warn him, without a doubt. They probably decided to loot the bank and clear out. Maybe they quarreled. Maybe Rudd just—eliminated him in order to get it all."

"Jason Rudd!" Linda shivered slightly. "To think that—! He seemed such a timid little man; it's hard to imagine him a wanton killer."

"These meek fellows often turn out to be holy terrors. If Rudd's cornered, he'll fight like a rat." Jim was watching the doorway, his gun drawn. He spoke without turning. "Linda, look through his desk. Examine everything. Although we know he's guilty, right up to this minute we haven't a bit of actual proof."

He continued to watch the doorway while she examined the contents of the desk. "Here are two guns," she said. "A big one and a little one with two barrels."

He nodded. In a bank it was customary to keep guns in desk drawers. He heard the rustle of papers as she moved them about, heard her thumb through books of account. Then she fave a stifled scream.

A voice said, *"Don't move!"*

Despite the command, Jim's head snapped around. One of the doors of the vault had swung outward and in the opening stood Jason Rudd.

It was his appearance rather than the gun which covered them that held them. It wasn't hard to recognize him as a killer now. His usually neat attire was disarranged, his sandy hair disheveled; the pasty face was harshly seamed and rigidly set, the lips parted and drawn. Between them they caught the gleam of his teeth. His eyes were wild and staring; he looked just what he was—a rat, cornered and desperate to the point of madness.

Jim spoke, stalling for time. "So that's where you were! Inside the safe. That's probably where you hid after you shot Dunham."

"*Shut up!*" The words fairly crackled. "Drop your gun."

Randall opened his hand and allowed the gun to fall.

"Linda, pick it up by the barrel and bring it to me. And don't get between him and me or you'll have an accident."

Linda looked at Jim, appeal in her eyes. He shook his head. "Do as he says."

"You're sensible," said Rudd. "I mean every word I say. Everything to gain and nothing to lose, you know. Fetch it here, Linda, and hand it to me butt first.... That's right." He moved sideways to his right, holding both guns now. "Put your hands up, Randall. Keep them there. Linda, go into the vault. You'll find two sacks. Bring them out and put them on the floor halfway to the door. Don't make a mistake or I'll shoot Randall first and then, if necessary, you."

Slowly she disappeared inside the vault. Randall tensed, hoping that Rudd would divide his attention for a moment, but the man kept both guns trained on him and his gaze did not falter. Linda came out carrying two sacks which she obediently deposited where he had directed.

"Now," said Rudd, "you will return to the vault and remain there. You, Randall, will follow her. I'll need both your horses."

"You're going to lock us inside."

"That's right. But I'll be generous; I'll not bind or gag you."

"Very generous! We can't claw our way through steel and a yell wouldn't be heard three feet away. Look here, Rudd, leave Linda outside. Tie her up good and tight and gag her so she can't make a sound, but don't lock her in that vault."

"That wouldn't fit in with my plans at all. Get inside, Linda."

"But good gosh, man, she'll suffocate! Her father is the only one left who knows the combination and he's out in the hills searching for her. It may be a day, two days, before they can fetch him here!"

"If they think of the safe at all, Randall. You get the idea perfectly. Inside with you, Linda. Hold it, Randall! Get those hands up again! Don't move an inch. If you force me to shoot I'll make a good job of it, I promise you. You first, then Linda. Get inside, Linda."

She turned her head and looked long at Jim, and in her eyes he read a message. She dropped her head, moved submissively towards the safe. Randall crouched slightly, muscles tense, concentrating on holding Rudd's entire attention. She had something in mind, some plan of action, and he must be prepared to move in a split second. Rudd thrust forth his head and cocked both guns.

She passed within four feet of him, feet moving reluctantly, and when she was a yard beyond him she turned and leaped. Her desperate fingers fastened on his arm, jerked him off balance. He uttered a ratlike squeal which was drowned out beneath the reports of both guns; then her arms were about him and he was surging and heaving like a suddenly released spring, the random shots from both guns striking furniture and walls and floor.

As she leaped, Jim leaped also. He sprang for the desk and seized the drawer which held the guns. So hard did he jerk it that it came clear out of the desk and the guns dropped to the floor. He felt the burn of a bullet across his shoulder as he dived for them.

It seemed that the devil himself was aiding Rudd. It was dark beneath the desk and Jim's fingers seemed all thumbs. Another bullet claimed his hat, a third tore off the heel of his boot, still another ripped through the desk above him. He had to lie flat in order to feel about for the guns.

While he fumbled he flung a glance towards them. Linda had locked her wrists across Rudd's chest and he was flinging her about like an empty sack, hammering with the heavy gun barrel at her wrists as he did so. And all the while he was uttering those little squeals of rage and terror. Her hold finally gave and she was flung to the floor. Instantly Rudd wheeled and jerked up his right hand gun, but he had emptied it in his wild shoothing and only a futile click sounded as the hammer fell.

Then Randall's right hand touched metal!

His gaze was riveted on Jason Rudd. The mad little man flung the empty gun at Linda, but she moved her head and it did not strike her. Swiftly changing the other gun to his right hand, Rudd started to raise it.

Randall fired, lying flat on the floor. It was a snap shot and at a difficult angle, but it struck Rudd in the leg and he came down to his knees. Supporting himself with his left hand, he raised the gun again; then Jim's second bullet struck him and he shuddered at the impact. Before he could regain his steadiness a whole volley sounded from the doorway and he went down like a wet rag.

Men were surging into the room, the sheriff in the lead, his big gun still smoking. Jim gave a sigh of thankfulness and pushed himself to his feet. He helped Linda up; she was white-faced and trembling.

"Are you all right, darling?" he asked anxiously.

She nodded. "It's not me, it's you. Jim, your coat is torn and there's blood on it. Oh, you're hurt, you're hurt!"

They removed his coat and sat him in a chair, and Tiny made a quick examination. "You'll need some hemstitchin'. Idaho, fetch the *medico*; he can crochet my scalp at the same time."

So once more Jim had a doctor work on him while an anxious-eyed Linda held his hand. And when it was over she naturally asked the question she had asked on a former occasion. "He'll be all right, Doctor?"

"Sure he will. By morning he'll be asking for—"

"A steak and hashed brown potatoes?"

"Why, yes. How did you know what I was going to say?"

"They been through it before, Doc," said the sheriff. "It's a long story but right interestin'. Some day when I got more time I'll tell you about it.... Well, we finally got this mess straightened out. Next thing is to find Mr. Lane and tell him his daughter's safe."

"Poor Dad!" sighed Linda. "I guess we'll have to go back East now. The Star will go back to Jim, and the bank—"

"Nothing wrong with the bank," said Jim quickly. "Financially sound and ready to go, with Brent Wood as bookkeeper and cashier. Your father'll make a mighty good president. And I'm sure he won't want to go back East and leave his only daughter."

She didn't answer, but the high color in her cheeks and the downcast eyes told him that she understood. She helped him on with his coat, buttoning it over the useless arm. Then came the clatter of tiny hoofs, and an excited "Whoa!" and Scotty came running into the room. His eyes were bright and excitement was written all over his seamed face. In his hand he grasped a much wrinkled telegraph blank.

"By gob, here you are!" he cried at sight of Jim. "I been huntin' all over the earth for you! This telegram come on the evenin' stage, and say! we been fooled from the start! It wasn't Lew Dunham that shot your pa and looted the bank. Know who it was? *Jason Rudd!*"

The consternation he had expected to arouse did not materialize. Jim grinned and said. "We know, old-timer. What's left of him is under that blanket over there."

Scotty's little eyes blinked. He walked over to the blanket and raised it. "Well—I'll—be—!" He dropped the blanket. "And I been chasin' all over—! How'd it happen?"

Tiny and Sam and Juan told him, and while they were about it Jim and Linda went out into the night. It was still dark, but above them the stars blinked benignly and the air was soft and caressing. The magic of it gripped them and they halted to look up and breathe deeply of the pine fragrance from the nearby hills. Jim's right arm slipped about her waist and as naturally as though it had always been thus her left arm circled him.

"It's wonderful!" she said softly. "So vast and quiet and yet so stirring. I love it. Jim, I never want to go back!"

"It gets into the blood," he said gravely. "I could never live anywhere else."

For some minutes they stood there in silence, then she turned to him.

"We must find Dad and tell him. And by the time we reach the Star it will be daylight. Are you ready for that steak and hashed brown potatoes?"

With a finger he lifted her chin so that the starlight was reflected in her eyes. "I'm a funny fellow," he said. "I was the despair of my mother because I always insisted upon having my dessert first."

He bent over and kissed her on the lips.

www.ingramcontent.com/pod-product-compliance
Lightning Source LLC
Chambersburg PA
CBHW020913180626
46816CB00007BA/2378